Palmer Jackson
Yankee Mountain Man

John Snider

Copyright Notice

Palmer Jackson: Yankee Mountain Man

First edition. Copyright © 2022 by John Snider. The information contained in this book is the intellectual property of John Snider and is governed by United States and International copyright laws. All rights reserved. No part of this publication, either text or image, may be used for any purpose other than personal use. Therefore, reproduction, modification, storage in a retrieval system, or retransmission, in any form or by any means, electronic, mechanical, or otherwise, for reasons other than personal use, except for brief quotations for reviews or articles and promotions, is strictly prohibited without prior written permission by the publisher.

This is a work of fiction. Names, characters, businesses, places, events, locales, and incidents are either the products of the author's imagination or used in a fictitious manner. Any resemblance to actual persons, living or dead, or actual events is purely coincidental.

Cover and Interior Design: Derinda Babcock

Editor(s): Jessica Tanner

PUBLISHED BY: John Snider, P.O. Box 3373, Pagosa Springs, CO 81147, 2022

Library Cataloging Data

Names: Snider, John (John Snider)

Palmer Jackson: Yankee Mountain Man / John Snider

160 p. 23cm × 15cm (9in × 6 in.)

ISBN-13: 979-8-218-02234-1 (paperback) | (ebook)

Key Words: Frontier & Pioneer Western Fiction, Western Fiction Classics, and Old West History of the U.S.

ACKNOWLEDGMENTS

First, I'd like to thank my wife for her research and support of my storytelling. Then, I'd like to thank my friend Jessica for her editing and help in getting this story in print. Next, I'd like to thank Derinda Babcock for creating my cover and formatting my story so it could be published and reach readers. I'd also like to thank my friends and family for pushing me to write down my tall tales. And last but not least, I'd like to thank my readers for picking up *Palmer Jackson: Yankee Mountain Man*.

CHAPTER ONE

Palmer Jackson was curled up under a wool blanket and a ragged piece of canvas. A fresh blanket of snow covered everything. If it had not been for the two mules steaming up the brisk mountain air as they stood between a couple of *piñon* trees you never would have known that anyone was around.

Palmer readied his thoughts for the coming day. The previous day he'd dodged two different groups of Indians. No idea who they were. They could have been Ute, Apache, or Comanche. It did not matter in this wild land who they were. Usually a lone white man was dead if he was unlucky enough to be located by a party of Indians. And Palmer knew that with the fresh snow he would be making a trail a blind man could follow.

He stuck his right arm out and gripped the corner of the canvas, pushing it up and over to throw the snow off and keep his two rifles and two pistols dry. His rifles, both Harris made flintlocks, he had a gunsmith in St. Louis, Missouri convert to the new percussion caps. He'd traded twelve beaver plews for the two percussion cap pistols.

To survive in this country a man needed to be mobile, formidable, and—if possible—invisible. You had to be aware of more than Indians because the Mexican people had just fought Spain for their independence and won. They were very wary of Americans moving into their country and taking what they had fought so hard for.

Palmer figured he was in what the Mexicans referred to as New Mexico. He had crossed a small river he was sure was the Pecos River. He had watered the mules and drank all that he could. Then he moved up a small *arroyo* about a mile and set up a dry camp.

As he dressed on this snowy morning, in wool shirt and wool britches, he looked at his boots; both had holes in the soles. Not wanting to get his feet any wetter than necessary, he dug in one of his leather panniers and found a pair of calf high moccasins. They had been well rubbed with bear grease, still he knew that they would not remain dry very long in the snow.

Dressed, he rummaged around in his possibles and pulled out a pack of deer jerky and another of dried prunes and raisins. This was breakfast. He didn't dare light a fire because the Indian bands were roaming about.

He hobbled one mule, a Jasper, and let him graze while he finished his meal. If he'd turned both mules loose, they probably would have left the country—leaving Palmer Jackson afoot. Mules were rather social animals, one always making sure that the other one did not leave him behind. Palmer cussed the mules because every time that they saw anyone—Indians, Mexicans, or whites—on horses or mules they would try to bray at them.

Yesterday, he had to jump off and grab the mules by their muzzles to keep them from braying at each group of Indians. Calling them no good, long-eared, sorry sons-of-bitches, he promised to trade them for horses at the first chance that he got. He had traded a small keg of rum and five pounds of powder for them in St. Louis and had known better. He should have had his ass kicked for trading for the two.

Palmer Jackson: Yankee Mountain Man

He finished his jerky, prunes, and raisins and washed it all down with a large drink of rum. Then, he caught up the loose mule, a Sally, and tied her, hobbled the Jasper and turned him loose to graze while he gathered his camp up in preparation of packing.

He filled his panniers with his possibles while waiting for the Jasper to graze a little longer. The snow melted rapidly and his feet already felt the damp.

The Jasper lifted his head and looked to the west.

Suddenly, Palmer smelled wood smoke.

Gathering the Jasper, he quickly threw the packsaddle and panniers on him, taking time to lash it down securely. He did not want to lose any of his equipment if he had to run for it. He put his riding saddle on the Sally, and then checked his firearms. He made sure the caps were still on the nipples and sealed with beeswax. He stuck his two pistols in his belt along with his Green River knife before he hung one rifle off of the saddle horn and settled the other across his lap. His powder horn and small possibles bag hung across his left shoulder. He kept everything as ready as he could because he knew that most of the time there was no second chance when things got tight.

He saddled and mounted the Sally, and let the other mule follow. He eased down and around the mountain, staying in the trees as much as possible. Palmer knew that he was still quite a ways from any settlement so this much smoke meant either an Indian camp or a large *ranchero* was near. He spent quite a bit of time easing in close enough to see the smoke sifting up through the trees.

Palmer dismounted and tied up the mules. He took both rifles with him as he eased closer to the smoke.

Palmer finally found a hole in the brush and looked. It had been a little ranchero, sod building for livestock, little sod house with the roof that was still smoldering. He could see the body of a man hanging upside down from a small cottonwood tree. There was some blackened wood under the man's head. One of the Indians' favorite things to do to their male victims after scalping them was to hang them upside down and light a fire under their head.

Palmer stood in the shadows for almost an hour before he cautiously ventured out into the clearing. A movement by the sod house brought his rifle to his shoulder. With his heart beating rapidly, he watched as a brown and white dog appeared. All Palmer could think of was that the goddamn dog had damn near made him dirty his britches.

Two cows lay dead behind the little barn. It looked like all that the Indians had taken were their tongues. If there had been any horses or other livestock around, they must have driven them away.

He walked cautiously around the building looking for anything to salvage since the poor, dead bastard couldn't use anything anymore. But it appeared the goddamn Indians had taken everything worth salvaging.

Palmer watched as the brown and white dog scratched at the bottom of the back wall of the little sod house. Then, he circled the place again. If there had been anyone else, the Indians must have hauled them off too.

Walking back around the house he noticed the dog sitting by the back wall. Talking softly, he slowly walked towards the animal. The closer that he got the more agitated the dog became. Palmer was about ten foot away when he noticed a couple of boards with scratches on them. What the hell was covered up there?

He took another step and the dog started towards him snarling. When he got closer, he touched the dog with the barrel of his rifle and then kicked him as hard as he could in the ribs. The dog never yelped or quit snarling, but he did back away.

Palmer Jackson: Yankee Mountain Man

It would probably be suicide to shoot the dog. Every Indian within five miles would probably hear the gun shot.

Palmer got close to the wall, reached down, and pulled one of the boards up.

There was a hole underneath. Palmer reached down and picked up the other board, as he lifted it up, he saw something move and he quickly aimed his rifle into the hole. As the dust settled, he saw a small face looking up at him. Goddamn Mexican had been smart enough to have an emergency hidey hole in case of an Indian attack.

Palmer realized he was looking at the tear-stained face of a boy around ten or eleven years old. The snarling goddamn dog came back and tried to climb in the hole with the boy. Palmer backed off and squatted in the shade of the wall.

There was some scurrying around in the hole and suddenly the boy's head popped up and swung around until he locked eyes with Palmer. The boy's face was covered with dirt. He stared at Palmer for a good minute before he started to climb out of the hole. The damn dog was close behind and when his head poked above the hole he snarled at Palmer again.

As soon as the boy was clear of the hole, he ran to the cottonwood trees nearby with the dog right on his heels.

Palmer was still squatting in the shade when he noticed a hand sticking out of the hole. Crossing back over, he glanced down at a woman covered with dirt trying to crawl out of the hidey hole. Palmer reached down and grabbed her by the arm and dragged her up and out of the hole. As soon as she was released, she started babbling in Spanish.

Palmer had no idea what she was saying. He tried to calm her down by telling her, "You are okay. You are okay."

She swiveled her head, desperately looking around. When she spied the man hanging upside down over the dead fire, she began shrieking a name over and over as she ran to where he was hanging. "Enrique, Enrique, Enrique."

Palmer hurried over and grabbed her by the shoulder. "Goddammit, woman, shut the fuck up. The fucking Indians are going to hear you." It did nothing to calm the frantic woman and she began to fight Palmer. He punched her on the tip of her chin to shut her up quickly. As she collapsed, he wondered whether the Indians were close enough to have heard the woman's screams.

He quickly went to where he had hidden the mules and rapidly led them into the little rancheros' yard. He stood his rifles against the tree the body was hanging in and then bent to pick up the woman in an attempt to get her on the pack mule. The two mules were boogery over the dead man hanging in the tree and kept side-ling away from Palmer as he attempted to slide the woman across the packsaddle and panniers, but he wound up dumping her onto the ground. Palmer grabbed the lead rope on the pack mule, reached down, and picked up the mule's left front leg, making him bend his leg at the knee, then he wrapped the lead rope around it leaving the mule immobile for the moment. Palmer picked the woman up again and softly cussed the mule as he sidled up to him. He heaved her up and across the panniers, balanced her the best that he could, and, using some leather string to lash her to the panniers, left her ass sticking up in the air. Palmer muttered, "Shit, lady, I don't think you missed many fucking meals."

Jerking the lead rope from the mule's front leg, Palmer then led him over to the other mule. Retrieving his rifles, he then swung up into the saddle. He could feel his hair stand and prickle on the back of his neck. Palmer figured that the Indians had to have heard the commotion and that he didn't have a hell of a lot of time to clear out before they came back.

Palmer Jackson: Yankee Mountain Man

Riding into the trees in the direction the boy and the dog had taken, he struck their tracks in the snow and quickly urged the mules forward. The tracks ended at a large piñon tree with the brown and white dog lying at the base.

He spurred his mule up next to the tree and saw the boy sitting on a limb about ten foot above the ground. Seeing the boy's frightened face, he tried to act calm and go slow. Speaking softly, he tried to relay to the child the urgency of the situation. "Boy, you need to get your skinny little ass down from there. We don't have a hell of a lot of time before those bastards come back. I know that you're probably scared plumb shitless as am I, but there is a hell of a good chance that the Indians heard your mom raising Cain a while ago and there's a good chance they're coming back to see what they forgot. And, son, I know that I'm getting to be a pretty old bastard but I still don't want to lose my hair to a goddamned Indian today."

Palmer held his arm up, reaching for the boy, who suddenly jumped into his arms. He damn near lost his seat and his rifle as the mule ran sideways because the boy's jump had surprised her along with Palmer. Swinging the boy behind him on the mule, he pointed them to the south and the west. They reached the top of the ridge about a quarter of a mile from the little ranchero and turned to look back. He saw eight or ten horsemen streaming down the ridge above the ranchero.

Turning the mule around and digging his heels into her belly, he headed straight west away from the sun. Palmer said, "Boy, if you value your hair, you better hold tight. Them red bastards are going to make a try for us and if we don't rustle our hocks, we're not gonna make it outta here with our hair."

The big riding mule started in a ground covering lope with the pack mule following.

JOHN SNIDER

Palmer said, "Goddamn it, boy, I hope we got your mom tied on good 'cause we don't have time to check."

CHAPTER TWO

"HAUW mule," he hollered, as there was no reason to go quietly now. He had the mule loping for about ten minutes when he saw some cattle running loose. They topped a small rise and could see a group of buildings about a half a mile away. Palmer looked back and saw that the Indians had come within a couple of a hundred yards of them. As his riding mule cleared a small arroyo, he heard the boy cry out. Looking back, he saw that the pack mule had stumbled, gone down, and lost the woman.

"Goddammit!" He jerked his mule to a stop. Jumping off without thinking, he pulled the boy off and handed him the second Harris rifle. Glancing towards the woman sprawled in the mud, Palmer decided she was either still unconscious or dead. He reached down grabbed the riding mule's front leg, picked it up, and then pulled the saddle horn towards himself causing the mule to fall over on her side in the mud. Pulling his Green River knife from his belt, he slit the mule's throat and held her down until she quit struggling. He then grabbed the woman by the arm and drug her behind the dead mule. Grabbing the boy, he took the second rifle from him and made him lay down next to the woman.

Still standing, Palmer pulled his rifle to his shoulder just as the Indians slid their horses across the muddy arroyo.

Palmer's first shot took the lead Indian off his horse as if he had hit a wall. Pulling his pistols, Palmer ducked the swing of an ax as he fired, almost touching the man's face. He fired the other pistol into the mass of bodies and horse flesh not knowing if he had scored or not.

His knife in one hand and the small ax that the Indian had dropped in the other, he turned to face the remainder of the Indians. Two of them had dismounted and were coming in a dead run when he heard a gunshot and one of them fell down. The other Indian had a puzzled look on his face, looking around, trying to locate the source of the shot. Palmer took a step forward and threw the ax that he had picked up at the Indian, sticking him in his shoulder, and making him drop his knife. He had a club of some kind in his other hand with which he took a swing at Palmer. Palmer swiped his Green River knife at the Indian's stomach. He lunged at Palmer swinging his club wildly. Palmer raised his left arm to block the swing, and the club struck him between the shoulder and the elbow. It hit with a sickening crunch as Palmer's knife stuck in the Indian's ribcage. Palmer went to his knees as the Indian jerked free and raised his club to strike again. Palmer lifted his uninjured arm to block the blow, but it never came. The Indian melted to the ground, and as he rolled over, Palmer saw the boy pull the ax back for another strike at the Indian's head.

Palmer struggled to his feet and noticed three other Indians riding away. He turned back around and could see men with rifles converging on them. As he watched the approaching men, he could hear the ax splatting against the Indian's skull. Turning back around, he reached with his good arm and took the ax from the boy, telling him that the Indian was dead and was no longer a threat to them.

The boy never said a word, but lifted his tear-stained face up. Palmer hugged the boy with his good arm. Then, six or seven men tried to get Palmer to sit down. One of them grabbed him by the bad arm. Suddenly dizzy, Palmer groaned and sat down heavily on the muddy ground. *Goddamn, that hurt like hell, I wonder if I pissed my britches.* Then he passed out.

The next thing that Palmer remembered was a fat man leaning over him. He tried to get up but found that several pairs of hands were holding him down. The fat man was holding a saw in his hand and babbling in Spanish at him. It suddenly occurred to Palmer that the fat son of a bitch was going to saw his fucking arm off. With a great roar, he began kicking and thrashing and found that one of the bastards had him around the neck, choking the shit out of him. Suddenly, they began backing off and became silent.

Coming up off the table that they had him on, he noticed that someone, holding one of his pistols, stood next to him. It was the boy. He was crying again but the pistol was steady. Palmer took the weapon from the boy and noticed that the pistol was cocked but had no cap on the nipple. The little fucker had bluffed all of them.

The fat Mexican started babbling at him again and Palmer tried to convey to them that he did not understand a goddamn word that they were saying. He started to leave and his arm hit the door jamb and pain exploded up his left side. He knew that his arm was probably shattered, but, by God, it was still hanging on his body.

As he stepped outside, he could see the boy's mom lying in the shade of the building with her head at an unusual angle. Must have happened when the shit-headed mule tripped and fell. It sure seemed like when you fell in a barrel of shit and you splashed around in it trying to get out that you splashed shit on quite a few other people.

Damn, he needed a drink. Palmer walked over to the pack mule. The mule was standing next to a tree, tied up. He began feeling around in the left-hand pannier with his good arm and fished out his small cask of rum. He sat the rum, about a two-gallon cask, on top of the panniers and tried to pull the wooden plug out one handed. The mule shied around, and the cask hit the mud next to the tree.

Palmer knew that if his pistol had been loaded that he would have shot the crazy bastard where he was standing. One of the men picked up the cask of rum and pulled the plug out. Another brought a wooden cup and filled it with Palmer's rum. He handed the cup to Palmer who slugged the entire cup down without breathing. He put down the empty cup and roared, "Waugh! Goddamn."

All the men jumped and backed up.

Palmer started talking, not caring if they understood him or not. "Someone has got to take care of the boy. I cannot stay here. I have got to get someone to set my arm. Nobody is going to cut that bastard off while I am still alive."

They all looked at him blankly as he spoke and pointed to the west. One man said, "Santa Fe?" When Palmer nodded. The man held up two fingers and acted as if he was walking. Pointing to the north, he told Palmer, "Taos" and held up one finger.

Palmer, pantomiming shooting, made them understand that he wanted his firearms. One man ran to another building and returned with one rifle and one pistol. Palmer cussed, poured himself another cup of rum, swallowed about half of it, and then told them that he wanted his other Harris rifle. The boy came around the building carrying the other Harris. He also had his possibles bag with the powder, balls, and caps.

The first thing that Palmer did was attempt to charge his weapons, but he couldn't do it one handed. The boy watched him fumble around and then took them from him and began charging them. He got powder and ball in all four firearms but couldn't understand about the percussion caps as all that the boy had ever seen were flintlock firearms. Palmer felt in the possibles bag and found the small bag that contained his percussion caps. Slowly and painfully, he put a cap on each weapons' nipple. He would have to worry about the beeswax later. He put one pistol in his belt and stuck the two Harris rifles and the other pistol in the panniers. He picked up the mule's lead rope and started towards the north—and hopefully Taos.

Palmer took about ten strides leading the mule when the goddamn brown and white dog rose from the mud where he had been laying and advanced towards him snarling. The mule shied back and to the side, jerking him from his feet. When he hit the ground, white-hot pain engulfed his whole being and blissfully everything went black.

Palmer woke up and everything was floating and flying around him. The only thing that was real was the boy and an old woman. She was chuckling and smiling, or trying to smile, but she appeared to only have about one or two teeth in her mouth. He struggled to get up, but the old lady cackled and pushed him back down, and then smeared a green paste into his mouth and on the inside of his cheek. He slowly relaxed and the god-damnedest things began happening.

His brother suddenly appeared. Hell, he'd been dead damn near twenty years or so. Yet there he was talking to Palmer. What was he saying? "Speak up, Quentin, I can't hear you."

Suddenly, the black half-breed woman he had wintered with up on the Green River three winters ago appeared. She was smoking her goddamn pipe and laughing at him. Goddammit, he was glad that he had gotten rid of her. He had traded her to a little French trapper by the name of Blue. He should have asked for more, but what the hell, five gallons of alcohol—that was worth something.

Damn, suddenly light was blinding him. *What kind of a fucking dream am I having now?* A fat man grinned at him and Palmer's first thought was MY ARM. *Sorry bastards are going to try cutting my arm off again.* Palmer began struggling and shouting. "Get away from my arm, you fat bastard."

There was a voice in broken English telling him to relax, his arm was still there. Palmer reached across his body with his good arm and could feel sticks and bandages. Then, there was the old lady back again with some more green shit and Palmer went back into the world of dreams and floating. *Hell*, he thought, *it's like I'm flying!*

CHAPTER THREE

He came to and, before he opened his eyes, he knew that he was laying in the sun. Damn, if it didn't feel good. When he opened his eyes, he could see clouds scudding across a blue sky. He mumbled, "Shit! I can smell fresh bread cooking. Damn, I haven't smelled fresh bread in twenty years or so. Maybe the old lady killed me and I've gone to Hell."

Palmer felt warmth and a little movement next to him. He turned his head slowly and looked down to see two little black eyes looking steadily up at him. The boy stood up and, as he did, the brown and white dog stood up also and began growling deep in his throat at Palmer.

Remembering his arm, he reached across his body with his good arm and felt the sticks again. He looked down to see that his left hand was still attached.

The boy turned and ran into the little building they had been laying against. Palmer struggled to sit up and he managed to lean his back against the building. Trying to catch his breath, he tried to regain a sense of what exactly had happened to him.

The old lady of his dreams appeared around the corner of the building and all that he could think was *no more of the green shit.* Palmer was struggling to get up when two men came trotting around the building, one of them was saying, "No, *señor*! No! No!"

Palmer thought, *Fuck them. I'm getting out of here.* When he made it up to his knees, his balance left him, and he started to pitch forward. One of the men caught him and let him lean back against the side of the building again. His equilibrium gone, his breathing rapid and shallow, he suddenly realized that he was weaker than a little girl. A little pussy was what he had become.

Three men and the old lady were standing in front of him. The men talking amongst themselves and the old lady smiling her toothless smile when another man began pushing his way through the others speaking in a quiet voice. "Pardon, señors, pardon." He stopped before Palmer.

Damn, there was the fat man from the dreams with the boy standing beside him. "Ah, señor, you are awake. We thought that perhaps God had decided to take you from us," the fat man said in very broken English.

Palmer started to ask him where he was and what in the hell had happened but when he attempted to talk his throat was so dry and tight that he could only croak and grunt. The fat man spoke, and the boy ran off. He returned quickly with a wide mouthed pottery jug. He went to his knees beside Palmer and put the jug to Palmer's lips. Water—cool, sweet, tasting water. Holy shit, he was thirsty.

The fat man said, "Please, drink in moderation, señor. You have been very sick." Palmer again attempted to stand, and the fat man grabbed him by his good shoulder and told him, "Please, señor. All in good time. You have been unconscious for almost one month. You have been very, very sick."

Palmer croaked. "A month? Bullshit."

The fat man responded, "No, no, the boy and the *bruja* have been taking care of you ever since you lost your senses."

Palmer Jackson: Yankee Mountain Man

Looking down, Palmer realized that he had no britches on—he was naked from the waist down. Palmer instinctively moved his good hand down to cover his privates and that made the old lady start laughing again. The fat man made a sign to the boy. The boy left and returned with a tattered blanket that looked a lot like Palmer's. After he covered Palmer's legs with the blanket, he looked up at the fat man as though asking for some help.

The fat man motioned the boy to his side and then began talking. "Señor, my name is *Padre* Ortiz. This village is called San Pedro as is the small stream running through the village. It is now in the winter of the year, and they have been caring for you here in the house of the lady *Señora* Dominguez. Señora Dominguez was once a great healer and now she is becoming quite forgetful as age takes its toll on her. She is still a fount of knowledge that we are trying to harvest as we can. We carry you outside and that way the boy will not have so much to clean up."

Palmer looked at the boy and then back to the priest. "You mean that the boy has been taking care of me, cleaning my shit and piss?"

"Yes," said the priest. "I must tell you that he has not left your side. He carries the pistol with him everywhere. Some of the men have tried to take the gun from him, but he continues to threaten the men if they persist in asking him to put down the gun."

Palmer looked at the boy with a whole different perspective, the little bastard had some balls. Been taking care of him for almost a month. Why no one had ever done that for him ever before! "My mule and my gear," Palmer asked.

The priest replied, with a smile, "The young man has all your belongings inside the building. Your mule grazes along the creek and the boy has five of the dead Indians' horses besides. They are hobbled with your mule." He pointed to the animals. "Señor, what name are you called?"

"Palmer," he replied, "call me Palmer."

The men repeated it several times.

"What is the boy's name?" Palmer said to the priest.

The priest replied, "The boy's name is Chavez. No one knows his given name and he refuses to speak. All of his family are gone—dead. His mother died in the fall of the mule and we journeyed to the ranchero of Chavez and found his father where he had been murdered. We buried both husband and wife behind the *casa* at the ranchero. I fashioned a cross for the graves and the boy has never cried or spoken of that. We know that you must have rescued Señora Chavez and the boy but are unaware of the circumstances. Señor Palmer, the soldiers from Santa Fe were here and wanting to know what had happened and how you happened to be in New Mexico. Señor, they are quite suspicious of Anglos."

"Well, Padre, hell with them. I'll be long gone in two days."

"Señor Palmer," the priest replied, "you are very weak and must not tax or tire your body overly much."

"Padre, I got to get going, I've been here way too long. Help me up, man. I've got to rustle my hocks out of here."

The priest helped Palmer to his feet and turned loose of him only to have to grab him as he fainted.

When he came to, Palmer was inside of the building, laying on a pallet stuffed full of dried grass. The boy was there, sitting by his side with the pistol on his lap. Palmer lay there a moment or two looking at the boy, then grinned at him, and said, "Goddamn boy, you got more sand and grit than most growed men, you ought to be a real tail twister in a few more years." The boy grinned back momentarily and then stood up and lay the pistol on Palmer's lap.

As the boy left the room, Palmer saw a brown and white shadow lying in the corner. The damn dog laying there, watching his every move. At least, he wasn't snarling and growling for the moment.

The boy returned with a wooden bowl of stew, more of a soup than anything. He advanced to Palmer's bad side and motioned for Palmer to sit up. The boy held his back until he could squirm against the wall. He then held the bowl against Palmer's lips and let him sip the liquid down. When Palmer got to the bottom of the bowl, there were a couple of gristly pieces of meat which he retrieved with the fingers of his good hand. "Goddamn, that meat tasted good." Palmer was thinking that, by Hell, he could eat a gallon of the stuff when he suddenly got a pain in his gut. He began trying to stand up, the boy had a panicked look on his face, and Palmer made it to his knees. He could not hold his bowels any longer and he sprayed shit all over the dirt floor. He began cussing—he had never been this weak. It had to have been the goddamn green paste that the old lady had been giving him. Christ, there the priest was standing in the doorway, a look of concern on his face. "Padre, you've got to help me out of here. I have never been in a spot like this before," Palmer said.

The priest said, "Señor Palmer, you must stay calm. The bruja says that you are much better, but you must be patient. She gave me this to make your bowels slow down." He was carrying a small, wooden bowl full of a black paste.

"Padre, she gave me that goddam green paste and I had some dreams that you would not believe."

The priest said, "The green paste was made from mushrooms that she gathers along the stream banks and they were to relax you and make you sleep. This is made from the charcoal of the fire and it will slow your bowels. You have eaten very little for a long time and she says that you must take nourishment very slowly or you will likely shit yourself to death."

Palmer tasted the black paste and made a face, and the priest urged him to finish it all. The boy came back in with a clay water jug and some rags and began cleaning Palmer. Palmer had never been so humiliated.

After the boy finished, Palmer beseeched the priest to help him stand. With his help, Palmer took a few steps and had to sit down on a stool that was against the wall. The boy came back in from washing the rags, and the dog who'd followed him out came back with him. The dog's hackles raised up when he saw Palmer and he started growling at him. The boy grasped the dog by the scruff of the neck and led him to Palmer's side. He had his lips raised in a snarl, but the boy took Palmer's hand and put it on the animal's head and began rubbing him while holding his hand on Palmer's hand. The animal quit snarling after a moment or two but remained very apprehensive as did Palmer. Palmer looked at the boy and grinned. The boy grinned back but said nothing.

The priest said, "Señor, the boy seems to relate quite well to you, but I am concerned about him not speaking."

Palmer replied, "Padre, I seem to remember that he's probably the only reason that this old man still has his left arm."

Padre Ortiz said, "Señor, your arm may not have been completely saved. We must remove the splints and bandages tomorrow and inspect your arm. It was crushed quite badly, and the old lady wrapped it and applied herb poultices to it every day. You had a great fever and were completely irrational. That is why she gave you the green mushroom paste so that you could sleep and rest. The boy stayed by your side all the time. He fed you broth and kept your body as clean as possible."

The priest produced another concoction of a brown color. "You must continue taking this. It is made of the bark of the willow tree. The old bruja said that you must eat more of the charcoal, the willow bark, and drink lots of water. She will feed you some goat stew and try to put some strength back into you."

"Padre," Palmer replied, "help me outside before I try eating again. I don't want to shit all over again."

The priest smiled and said, "As your strength returns, we will take you outside when possible. You must remember that winter is coming and it is becoming quite cold."

Palmer said, "Padre, I realize that I am mighty beholden to you, the old lady, and the boy, but I have got to get out of here. I can't spend the winter laying on my hind end, letting that boy clean up my messes." The priest smiled and told Palmer not to get in a hurry.

It was four more days before Palmer could stand by himself and walk outside. In an additional four days, he could walk to the creek and bathe himself, take a dump, and WIPE HIMSELF. On the tenth day, he caught the mule up and tried to saddle him. He couldn't hold him and get the saddle swung up on him.

Early the next morning, a hell of a commotion woke him up. After dressing, he stepped outside to see what was happening and saw that the boy had caught the mule up and somehow got him saddled. That was not what was causing all the ruckus. He had also caught one of the dead Indians' horses and was attempting to saddle him.

Palmer stood and watched the young lad fight the horse for several minutes. Then, he walked out and motioned for the boy to come to him. He spent a few moments trying to talk to the young man and finally gave up. Palmer started pantomiming, trying to show him that he wanted him to tie one of the horse's hind legs up. The boy finally grasped the idea of tying one of the horse's hind legs up. After a whirlwind of activity in a cloud of dust, the horse had a leg tied up in which the only help Palmer contributed was a mountain of cussing. The boy finally got the packsaddle on the Indian horse, put the panniers on, and put all of Palmer's meager possessions in the panniers, and then released the horse's hind leg. The little Indian horse immediately bucked everything off, including the panniers.

He continued pitching, bucking, and bawling until he became tangled in the rawhide rope and threw himself. Two of the village men had turned out to see what all the commotion was about and, when the horse fell, they promptly sat on his head, preventing him from rising again.

Palmer indicated to them to again tie the horse's hind leg up and to let him up once more. When the horse once again regained his feet, three feet, Palmer and the boy started gathering his possessions and distributing them into the panniers evenly. Once the panniers were loaded as evenly as they could determine, Palmer indicated that the two men should hang them on the cross-buck saddle.

After the panniers were loaded, he had the boy throw a ragged piece of canvas across both loaded panniers and the packsaddle. Then, Palmer took a piece of rope and, with the young boy's help, he secured the panniers with a diamond hitch. Once that was secured to Palmer's satisfaction, he indicated to the boy to release the horse's rear and front legs as they had to hobble the horse's front legs also.

Palmer Jackson: Yankee Mountain Man

As soon as the horse's rear leg touched the ground, he once again began to pitch and buck. He continued until he was just too tired to buck any more. At this point, Palmer had the boy climb on the saddled mule and then handed the boy the lead rope of the pack horse, indicating to the young man that he should wrap the lead rope around the horn of the saddle and then lead the horse around the outskirts of the village until he settled down. Within one hour, the horse was acting like a veteran pack animal.

Later that day, they hobbled and released the horse and mule to graze.

The boy and Palmer had a meal that the old lady fixed consisting of beans with pieces of goat meat and seasoned with ground red *chili*. As they ate, the priest knocked on the door and asked to enter. The old woman gave a bowl of beans with some goat meat to him. Palmer, the boy, and the old woman watched in awe as the priest seemed to just inhale the food.

The priest finished his second bowl, looked up at Palmer, and burped loudly. Palmer looked at the priest and laughed. The old lady laughed and the priest himself chuckled loudly. Palmer glanced at the boy and saw that he had finally smiled. The young man had not laughed, but he did smile.

The priest noticed also, but he did not comment. He looked at Palmer and said, "Señor, what are you to do with the boy?"

Palmer looked at him with a pained expression and replied, "Hell, Padre, I am not doing nothing with the boy!"

The priest was silent for a moment before saying anything. Then, rather forcefully, he spoke. "Señor, the other children are afraid of him. He has even threatened some of the adults. For one, the *alcalde* when he was to remove your arm. Some even consider him possessed because he cannot speak. He will not have a place if he stays here in this village."

"Padre, there is no possible way that I can take a young boy like him with me. Hell, the minute that I leave it's possible that I might have Indians after me." Palmer looked at the priest. "If that happens, he wouldn't last a heartbeat."

The priest was silent for a moment and then said, "Señor, if he stays here, he has no family, no friends, no one to care for him, and he seems to think that you and he belong together."

"Damn, Padre, both you and him get that notion out of your heads. I am leaving in the morning at first light and the boy stays," Palmer emphatically replied.

The priest said, "I hope you realize how this may affect this young man, but whatever. May God go with you on your travels."

CHAPTER FOUR

The next morning, at first daylight, Palmer had his mule saddled and the Indian horse packed. He had just finished packing when the priest showed up. He said, "Morning, Padre, I need you to do something for me, if you can." The priest repeated the morning greeting and asked how he could be of service.

Palmer said, "I'm leaving the other Indian horses for the boy. I'm also leaving the boy one of my pistols, a horn of powder, and a bar of lead." He also left one of his precious gold eagles with the priest for the old woman.

As he rode off towards the northwest, Palmer glanced back and saw that the priest still stood in the middle of the village square as the sun came up.

The first day, he didn't get more than ten miles up the little river before his wounded arm started hurting bad. He decided to stop along the river in a spot that he could hobble his livestock and make camp.

The next morning, as he was breaking camp, he noticed movement back the way that he had come. Quickly saddling his mule and getting the pack on the horse, he started to ease on up the river when a horse nickered behind them.

His riding mule brayed and his packhorse nickered an answer. Cocking his rifle, he pulled up to see what kind of a shithole that he had gotten himself in when to his surprise the young boy appeared, riding one of the Indian horses and leading three others.

No one appeared to be following the boy, so Palmer waited until he caught up to him and then started into cussing. "Goddammit, boy, can't you see that this is never gonna work? You gotta go back. Turn them goddamn horses around and get back to the village." Waving his arms and hollering, Palmer indicated that he wanted the boy to leave and return to the village.

The boy simply sat on his horse and stared at Palmer.

Palmer held his hand out to tell the boy to stop and then jerked his mule around and started on up the muddy little cart track. He traveled about two or three hundred yards and then looked back over his shoulder, and the boy was still sitting on his horse watching him disappear. *Maybe he'll get the idea that he needs to go back to the village*, Palmer thought. That night as he made camp, he saw something move in the brush. The brown and white dog walked out, sat down, and watched him for a time before fading back into the brush.

Right at twilight, Palmer's horse nickered, and he knew that the kid had to be close. Picking up one of his rifles and tucking his pistol into his belt, he started sneaking back down the trail. He hadn't gone over a quarter of a mile when he heard the dog growl. He stopped and looked around and he could see the four horses hobbled and grazing along the river. He looked further and could see the brown and white dog under a tree. Then, in the dim light, he saw the boy. He was lying next to the brown and white dog.

When he got closer, the dog started growling, the boy lay his arm over the dog, and he quieted. Palmer walked on up. The boy had on nothing but a shirt and pants. He had no shoes, no blanket, and he was shivering bad.

Palmer turned towards the horses, saying as he went, "Boy, let's get these goddamn horses up the river and eat something." Not knowing if the boy understood or not, Palmer started catching horses and taking their hobbles off. By the time that he had the hobbles off the second one, the boy had caught and removed the hobbles on the other two and was following Palmer up river.

When they got to Palmer's camp, they hobbled the four horses and turned them loose with the mule and the packhorse. Palmer walked over to his camp and started gathering some dry wood. He'd seen no sign of any Indians for the last two days, actually no sign of any humans at all. Palmer thought that it would probably be safe to have a fire and maybe warm the boy up a little. Palmer took his Green River knife and whittled a handful of pitch shavings off a piñon limb, crushed them up with a handful of moss off of a tree, reached into his possibles bag for his steel and flint, crouched down, held the flint and steel next to the pile of moss and shavings, and struck the steel to the flint. He had to repeat the process about three times before a spark started the moss smoldering. Gently blowing on the moss produced a finger of flame that ignited the pitch shavings. Slowly adding twigs to the tiny flame, the man and boy soon were adding larger branches to a warm, crackling fire.

Palmer had a battered, fire-blackened pot that he carried to the river and returned with full of water. As he placed it on the fire, he noticed the boy and the dog sitting together, backed away from the fire, and the boy was still shivering. Motioning for the boy to come forward, he gruffly spoke, "Goddammit, boy, come, warm up. I'll brew us some tea and we got us some prunes and some jerky."

The boy and the dog moved next to the fire.

Palmer went to his panniers, got a blanket, went back to the fire, and dropped the blanket around the lad's shoulders. The dog had moved up with the boy and he growled at Palmer when he dropped the blanket.

Palmer went to the other side of the fire and looked at the boy and his dog. Grinning at them, he spoke in a gruff voice. "Boy, I don't know if you can savvy what I am talking about, but we have got us a hell of a pee-dinger of a situation. I never been around a youngster like you before, and this is mighty tough country. If you two are gonna partner with old Palmer Jackson, we gotta get us some rules. 'Til we find us some more supplies. We got to pay attention to what we do."

About then the pot started simmering. Palmer went to the panniers and brought back three leather bags. He reached in one and drew out some tea which he threw into the steaming pot. He reached in the second bag and brought forth a handful of prunes. He lay them on a tattered piece of canvas. Reaching in the other bag, he brought out a handful of jerky. He handed two pieces to the boy who immediately gave one to the brown and white dog.

Palmer reacted explosively, "Damn, boy, that's your supper. Don't feed that brown and white son-of-a-bitch that jerky. It's still right at a hundred miles yet to Taos—and we might need it."

The boy, with no expression, looked at Palmer. Palmer looked at the boy with a very dark look for a few moments, then he sighed, and looked up at the stars. "Damn, boy, the whole world knows that I owe you. I probably wouldn't have this dammed left arm if it hadn't been for you, but I have never been around a child before, so you have got to give this old hoss just a little slack. Hell's fire! I don't even know if you can understand me. The priest said that he thought that maybe you had been scared so bad that you didn't want to talk. I am dammed sorry about your mama and your papa. If I'd been there a couple of hours sooner, I still couldn't have saved your papa. I probably would have lost my hair, too. As far as your ma went, we might have made it to San Pedro if that shit-headed mule hadn't fallen with her, but you just never know. I want you to forget about me hollering at you and the dammed dog and let's eat supper such as it is." Palmer reached in the jerky sack and withdrew another piece which he threw to the brown and white dog.

He grinned at the boy. "What the hell, we run out of grub, we can eat that brown and white bastard." Then he laughed so loud that it startled the hobbled horses for an instant. "Hell," he said, "I've eaten them before and thought they were purty fair."

Still chuckling, he removed the tea pot from the fire. He went back to the panniers, got a half a handful of sugar, and stirred it into the pot with his knife. After it had cooled for a few minutes, he picked it up, took a big swallow, and then threw back his head, growling out a loud, "Waugh!" It startled the boy and the dog. Palmer grinned at the boy and handed him the pot.

The boy took a big sip of the sweet tea, tipped his head back, and growled a loud, "Waugh."

Palmer threw back his head and laughed 'til he had tears running down his face. He looked over and seen that the boy was laughing also. It was at least a full minute before they got control of themselves. Palmer and the boy continued sipping tea and growling at each other until the pot was dry.

They gathered up all the pieces of bedding that Palmer could find, two blankets and another piece of canvas. The boy laid down next to the fire and Palmer covered him up with a blanket. Then, he walked to the other side of the fire, made sure his rifles and pistol were covered by the piece of canvas, and lay down. Palmer tried to sleep, but things were flitting through his mind. One thing that he had noticed about the boy was that he took care to have the pistol he'd given him close and covered to keep it dry.

A short time after the fire died, he felt movement and a small form lay down next to him. It was not long until he felt the brown and white dog lay down next to the boy. It was far into the early morning before Palmer Jackson could sleep because he was wondering what in the hell an old mossback like himself was going to do with a boy and a brown and white dog.

Daylight found Palmer stirring coals up and adding some moss to them. Blowing on the coals until a tiny flame sprang up, he started putting twigs on and soon had a nice little fire going. Reaching over and shaking the boy awake, he told him that it was time to travel. The boy never said a thing, but he did smile at Palmer.

The boy picked up the water pot, walked down to the stream, and filled it. Bringing it back to the fire, he nestled it amongst the coals and looked up at Palmer, watching him.

"Boy," Palmer said, "we usually don't heat water for tea, but, what the hell, this isn't usual either."

Palmer brewed another pot of tea. He and the boy breakfasted on tea, jerky, prunes, and raisins.

After they ate and warmed up a little, Palmer dug around in his possibles bag and pulled his boots out. He then took his moccasins off and put the boots on. Next, he dug out some rawhide string. Then, he motioned for the boy to hold his foot up. He took a moccasin and put it on the boy's foot. Using his fingers, he felt for the end of the boy's toes and then removed it. Taking his knife, he punched five holes top and bottom. Using the rawhide string, he laced both moccasins approximately the same. He plucked several handfuls of dry grass and stuffed the moccasins full of grass. Handing them to the boy, he indicated for him to put them on.

The boy put them on and attempted to walk with his new footwear. They were so long that he had to shuffle as he walked to be able to keep them on and not trip. Palmer chuckled at the young man's actions and said, "Hell, boy, not real pretty but warmer than what you had."

Catching up the horses and saddling took almost an hour as the two Indian horses had to have a leg tied up before they could be saddled and packed. By the time they were packed up, the sun was already steaming the ground.

Before they mounted, Palmer took the wool blanket that the boy had slept in and folded it in half. He took his knife and made a slit about one foot long in the center of the blanket. Palmer took the blanket to the boy and slid it over his head, making a poncho-like garment of the wool blanket to keep the boy warm. The two then mounted their critters and headed north once more. Palmer riding a mule and leading a pack horse, the boy riding an Indian horse and leading the other three Indian horses, who were tied head to tail. The brown and white dog ranged along the sides and at times in front. Palmer, looking back at the procession, had to smile at the little train behind him.

After two days along the muddy track, Palmer and the boy came up on eight oxcarts making camp. They stopped to talk to the drivers. Palmer and the boy were invited to make camp with them. Palmer figured that it was probably more to have his rifles with them than for the hospitality. One of the men understood and could talk a smattering of English. He helped Palmer to understand that he and the boy could eat with them.

The drover, who was cooking, gave them each a wooden bowl full of stew made from deer meat, beans, and red chilies along with a couple of pieces of flatbread baked on a large, flat rock by the fire. As they began to eat, the stew seemed like it was liquid fire to Palmer. Everyone else—even the boy—was eating as though it was great stuff. Determined not to be a quitter, he doggedly consumed the bowl. The cook indicated that he could have more. Palmer hastily declined. Going to his panniers, he rummaged around and found his pipe and a small bag of tobacco. After stuffing and lighting up his pipe with an ember from the fire, he offered his tobacco pouch to the head drover and indicated that he should pass it around.

The drovers accepted readily. Instead of pipes, they produced corn husks. They filled them with tobacco, rolled them, and smoked them like a cigar. They called them *cigarillos*.

Palmer still had about a gallon and a half of rum left in a cask. Retrieving the cask from one of the panniers, he returned to the fire. The head drover brought out a clean wooden bowl. Palmer filled the bowl with rum, took a swallow, and handed it to the drover. The man took a deep swallow and handed it to the next man. It took about three men to empty the bowl, and then Palmer would fill it again. This went on until the cask was empty. The drovers were laughing, a couple of them were singing some kind of Mexican song.

Palmer figured the boy and him better bed down in some trees down by a small creek, a seep more than anything, but it had enough water for them and all their stock. The boy and him picked out a dry spot under some pine trees and spread their tarp and blankets for bed. They checked their livestock, relieved their bladders, went back to the blankets, and made sure to cover everything with their canvas.

    Sometime later, Palmer woke and realized that it was snowing. Going back to sleep was hard to accomplish so he just lay there, not moving, thinking about the coming day. Suddenly, the dog growled low in his throat and stood up. Palmer retrieved his pistol from under his saddle and quietly sat up. As he sat up, the dog, snarling and barking, bolted into the trees.

CHAPTER FIVE

Grabbing his rifle, he ran barefoot after the dog and through the trees. He heard a shout of pain and then the dog yelped. As he came out of the trees, he could see three figures outlined in the snow trying to remove the hobbles on three of the horses. Palmer immediately threw up his pistol and fired at one. Without checking to see if he had hit the man, he stuck the pistol in his belt and fired his rifle at the other two. Knowing that he had struck one of the men, he continued to charge at the other. Whoever it was tried to swing aboard a plunging horse when a blur went by Palmer and pulled the man from the horse.

It was the boy's dog.

The dog had the man by the arm. The man threw the dog about as he struggled to free himself. When Palmer reached them, he struck the man in the throat with his rifle. He fell to the ground with a gagging sound. Palmer then struck him in the side of the head with the heavy Harris rifle.

As Palmer turned to check the other two, the first one that he had shot at had his own rifle and fired at Palmer. Palmer ran at the man, the bullet tugged at his left arm, but did not slow him. Just as Palmer was about to reach the man, the dog shot by him and grabbed the man by the thigh. Palmer drew back to club him with the Harris rifle, and a shot rang out from his right. The figure went down.

Palmer turned. Standing a short ways away was the boy with his other Harris rifle and his pistol tucked in his belt. The boy pulled the pistol from his pants and handed it to Palmer. He also had his possibles bag with powder and ball and immediately began charging the Harris rifle. As soon as he had charged the Harris, he put a cap on the nipple and handed it to Palmer. Palmer let him charge the other Harris rifle and the pistol while he investigated the figure on the ground.

The dog was still worrying the body when Palmer approached him and tried to calm him in a low voice. The dog stopped, looked up at him, then grabbed the body once more, and shook it. The boy crooned something to the dog as he finished charging the rifle and pistol. The dog turned the body loose again and backed away until he came to the boy. As Palmer got closer, he could tell that the body was an Indian. As he was poking him with the barrel of the Harris, figures started coming out of the trees where the oxcart drovers were camped. Two of the drovers, bearing arms, approached cautiously. Together they checked all the bodies and found them dead.

The drovers built the fire up and gathered around it. Palmer and the boy checked the horses and one mule, and found that the horse the one Indian had been trying to swing up on was wandering loose. They caught and re-hobbled it. They then joined the drovers at the fire to try to dry out. As they dried, they answered the freighters' questions.

Palmer noticed that the brown and white dog wasn't there. He whistled, but no dog came. He looked into the dark, but nothing. Looking at the boy, he said, "Call the dog, son."

Palmer Jackson: Yankee Mountain Man

The boy walked into the dark a short distance and called, "Chico, high, Chico." This was almost the first time Palmer had heard him speak since he'd met him. Again the boy called, "Chico, high, Chico." He walked into the snow and dark.

Palmer followed, his head swiveling, searching the dark-hued snow. He heard a sob and turned towards the sound. He could see the boy huddled over a form in the darkness. When he reached the boy, he could see that he was cradling the dog's head in his lap. He squatted down next to him and could see that the dog was laying with his eyes closed. He reached under the dog and picked him up. With the boy following, he carried the dog to the fire and laid him down.

The young lad squatted down next to the dog and then looked up at Palmer. "*POR FAVOR*! Señor Palmer, POR FAVOR!" The boy looked at him with a tear-streaked face.

Palmer squatted down next to the boy and checked the dog. He said, "Goddammit, boy that dog saved my ass and yours too. Look at his head and hip. Hell, boy, I feel bad, but I don't know what we can do."

The boy stood, walked off, and returned with his blanket and a small tarp. He covered the dog, sat down by him, and then looked up at Palmer. "POR FAVOR, señor."

The next morning the dog was still alive. Palmer talked to the drovers and got them to put the dog in one of the two wheeled carts. The boy and him gathered their horses and mule, packed up, and followed the slow-moving ox-drawn carts on their way to Taos.

About midday, the carts stopped before fording a small stream. The boy and Palmer approached the cart that was carrying the dog. Palmer raised the canvas and the dog poked his head out. The boy gave a small shout and climbed up on the cart with his dog. The dog was alert but did not want to get up. Palmer used various motions to signal to the drovers that he would like the boy to be able to ride with the dog. The drovers agreed, and Palmer tied the boy's horse to the cart. He then tied the other three horses head to tail and tied them to the packhorse's tail. Mounting his mule, he signaled that they were ready and followed the carts. At about dusk, they reached the village of Taos.

Palmer retrieved the dog and carried him towards a small *cantina* with the boy following. When he stepped inside of the cantina, silence blanketed the room. The bartender came around the bar saying, "No, señor, you can't come with a *perro*."

Palmer continued over to a vacant table and laid the dog on the floor by his chair. The boy had the two Harris rifles and one of the pistols. Palmer laid the rifles on the table, then he dug in his wool pants, and found one of his last gold Eagles. He laid it on the table with the rifles before he took the boy's pistol, made sure it was charged, and turned to the bartender. Palmer handed the boy's firearm back to him and then he motioned to the bartender to bring the boy something to eat. After seeing the gold coin, the bartender was smiling and very friendly. Palmer told the boy to stay with Chico. As he left, he turned and glanced back at the boy and smiled to himself because the boy was sitting at the table holding his pistol in his lap.

Palmer then found the oxcart drivers and, conversing with motions and a few words, had them corral his horses and mule with their oxen. He then carried the panniers and his few possibles back to the cantina.

As he entered, the conversation in the cantina came to an abrupt halt again. There were two bearded men hovering over the boy and the dog. Palmer could see that the boy was frightened but was holding his pistol cocked and steady with both hands. "Have we got a goddamn problem here, boys," Palmer asked in a loud voice.

The two men turned and looked at him. The smaller one spoke in English, "Just trying to help the boy, stranger. Just trying to help. No sense getting het-up about it."

Palmer realized the two were Anglos and sensed that they had been up to no good. Palmer replied, "Now, fellers, I'd be mighty careful about fucking with this boy and his dog. He's already laid out a couple of Indians with that there pistol of his. If he caint get the job done, well, I reckon Palmer Jackson will do it for him!"

"Damn, stranger! Don't get your damn back up! We didn't know he was with you."

Palmer glanced at the table and noticed that the gold eagle was gone. Looking up at the two men, he said, "You sons of bitches know anything about the coin the boy had?"

The smaller one dug into a pocket and produced a gold eagle. He told Palmer, "Hell, we was just keeping it so them Mex bastards wouldn't get it." He laid it on the table.

"We really appreciate your taking care of it for us," Palmer said, "but I don't think we're going to need your help anymore."

"No problem," the talkative one said as he and his partner moved towards the door.

After they cleared the door, Palmer heard the boy uncock his pistol. Palmer turned around and said, "Hell, boy, you did good, damn good." He squatted down next to the boy's dog and laid his hand on him.

The dog raised his head, but never tried to get up.

"Damn Indian purt-near did him in boy, but I think he's going to make out all right." He looked over at the innkeeper and said, "How about some grub?"

The man nodded and said, "Right away, señor. The boy too?"

Palmer replied, "Damn right, and the dog also."

All three of them cleaned their bowls of the rich stew consisting of meat, either deer or goat, and beans. Palmer also had a large flagon of warm beer. The boy and the dog drank water. After consuming their meal, Palmer made arrangements with the innkeeper to sleep in the livery stable in the back of the cantina.

Palmer carried the dog. The boy and the innkeeper followed with the weapons and their belongings. They exited through the rear door of the cantina and went into the barn. The innkeeper hung a lighted lantern in the barn. After setting down the dog, Palmer spread some fresh grass hay on the floor of a stall.

The innkeeper told them, "*Buenos tardes*, señors," and left them to their own devices.

Spreading their tarp on the hay, Palmer then spread their blankets on the tarp. Next, he picked up the dog and lay him at the foot of their bed on the fresh hay. He and the boy stood their rifles against the stall wall next to their heads. He told the boy, "Hell, boy, we're probably going to get spoiled living like this." They removed their foot-gear,

Palmer blew the lantern out, and they crawled into their bed.

It was probably after midnight when Palmer suddenly became aware of the dog growling softly. He sat up, cocked his pistol, and said into the darkness, "If you sorry bastards don't leave these .30 calibers are going to blow a hole in your rotten asses."

There was silence for half a moment, then there was the sound of footsteps leaving.

The dog quit growling and Palmer laid his hand on him saying, "That's two times, dog. Two times." He felt the boy move and then heard him uncock his pistol, also. Palmer said, "You'll do, boy. You'll do."

CHAPTER SIX

Just at daybreak, a rooster started crowing. Palmer sat up scratching his beard, belly, and other parts. He looked over at the boy and all he could see were two little brown eyes looking up at him. The boy's face and body were completely covered except for the hole he was peering through. Palmer said to him, "Let's get up and rustle something to eat, boy, and then we got us some dickerin' to do." They washed their faces and hands in a water trough at the front of the barn, and then they entered the cantina through the back door where they heard someone moving about.

They were greeted by a large woman who was stirring coals up in a large cook stove. "*Como esta,* señor?"

Palmer replied with a nod of his head. The boy spoke, "*Muy bueno*, señora. Señor Palmer *y mi querer comer,* por favor, señora."

She smiled at the lad before she motioned him and Palmer towards a table next to the stove. Soon the stove was radiating some welcome heat into the room.

The woman soon had a pot of beans steaming and was rolling and mashing dough into thin flat sheets that she then put on the stove top to cook. She then filled two large wooden bowls with the steaming beans and set them on the table in front of Palmer and the boy. As the bread cooked on the stove top, they hungrily started devouring the beans.

The beans had small pieces of meat in it that the boy tried to explain to Palmer was goat.

Palmer said between mouthfuls, "Hell, boy, I'm so damn hungry that I wouldn't care if it was polecat."

The woman handed each of them a bread off the stove and the boy again tried to explain to Palmer what they were eating. Pointing at the food, he told Palmer the chunks of meat were *cabras*, the beans were *frijoles*, and the bread was *tortillas*. Palmer grinned at the boy as he ate and said, "I know one word that'll work on a Mexican and that is 'Bueno, muy bueno.'"

The woman and the boy both smiled and said, "Bueno, muy bueno."

After consuming as much as they could, Palmer and the boy left a Mexican silver dollar for the woman and went to check on the boy's dog. Before leaving the cantina, Palmer begged a large bowl of table scraps off the woman for the boy's dog. The young lad sat the bowl down in front of the dog and watched him devour it in what seemed to be just seconds. With a large grin, the boy turned to Palmer and said, "Bueno, Señor Palmer. Muy bueno!" Gathering their panniers and possibles bag, the unlikely pair headed off to talk to the oxcart drovers and to check on the horses and mules.

Approaching the drovers, they were greeted with much hollering and laughter. The *carreta* men were still celebrating a successful trip with *mescal* and rum. Palmer turned down offers of rum for breakfast and told the captain that they were going to take the livestock and leave.

The captain told Palmer in broken English that they were leaving for Santa Fe in two days and that he and the boy were welcome to travel with them if they so desired. Palmer thanked him and told him that at the moment they were traveling north, if money and weather permitted.

Palmer Jackson: Yankee Mountain Man

Gathering the Indian horses, they saddled one, packed one, and saddled the mule. Then, Palmer asked the head drover who would buy horses. The drover told him that a man named Santiago owned the corrals and sheds where they corralled their livestock and *carretas* and that possibly he would be interested in buying or trading for the horses.

It was mid-morning by the time Palmer and the boy located Santiago who was already entrenched in a cantina and well on the way to becoming intoxicated. He informed them that he was not interested in purchasing their horses, but that a lady on the other side of the village was buying stock for a ranch that she had just purchased. With directions to locate the lady, they walked their animals down the street.

The village was coming alive and Palmer noticed that quite a few Anglos were present. Since Mexico had won their independence from Spain in 1821, it was welcoming trade and trade goods from the fledgling United States of America, especially in northern Mexico, or what was being called New Mexico. Pulling their goods from Mexico City or Chihuahua was too damn far and time-consuming. It was into this hub of activity that Palmer, a shaggy mountain man, an almost barefoot boy in threadbare clothes, and a limping brown and white dog met a person that would change their rapidly changing lives even more.

As they approached the building, they had been given directions to, Palmer could hear a loud ruckus coming from inside. Palmer and the boy tied the animals up to several trees by the side of the building which was quite obviously a large cantina and entered, carrying their firearms. As soon as they had entered, Palmer reached down with his free hand and pulled the boy into the shadows with him. As his eyes adjusted to the dark interior after being out in the bright sunlight, he could see three figures across the room from them.

There was a female sprawled across a portion of the floor with a trickle of blood coming from her nose. Carefully cocking his rifle, Palmer lay it across his arm and spoke. "I don't like to butt in on an argument, but we're looking for a drink and some grub."

One of the men swung around. The other one held a knife to the throat of a third man, who was bent backward over the long bar. The first cursed and attempted to level a rifle at Palmer and the boy.

As the man was cocking his piece, Palmer pulled the trigger on his Harris rifle, knocking the man to the floor. The other man, realizing that his partner was down, dropped his knife and grabbed at a small pile of gold and silver coins on the bar. Palmer rapidly drew his pistol from his waistband and fired at the man as he ran across the floor towards the back door. At the same time, he heard the boy's pistol go off. The man noticeably flinched but continued running through the back door and down an alley towards some trees. Palmer and the boy stopped in the alley. There, Palmer recharged his rifle and pistol, and then did the same for the boy's.

After recharging the weapons, Palmer and the boy reentered the building. The man that had been bent over the bar was huddled over the woman on the floor. Wiping the woman's face with a rag, the man, obviously the bartender, looked up at Palmer and gushed, "*Gracias*, señor! *Mucho gracias!* You have saved my life."

Palmer replied, "I hate to get involved, but I was looking for a lady that a man named Santiago said was looking to buy some horses."

The bartender replied that the señora was indeed looking for horses but was at this very moment lying on the floor unconscious. Palmer stepped back as men started to crowd into the cantina to see what the commotion was about.

Palmer Jackson: Yankee Mountain Man

One of the men, who the bartender called the alcalde, went to the body on the floor and rolled him over and as he did Palmer recognized that he was one of the bearded men from the night before at the other cantina and the confrontation with the boy. The alcalde spoke to the bartender in Spanish for a few moments and then approached Palmer with a smile. As he approached, Palmer became aware of the brown and white dog and realized that the animal had not left his and the boy's sides the whole time the incident had taken to play out. The dog was softly growling as the alcalde approached. Palmer motioned to the boy, who put his hand on the dog's head, and he stopped growling.

The alcalde smiled at Palmer and the boy and then spoke in English. "Sir, the bartender, Señor Gallegos, wishes to thank you and say that the Señora Barcelo would most certainly thank you for your intervention in this matter. He said that if you had not intervened he would probably be dead and Señora Barcelo would have been robbed and possibly worse."

Palmer replied that he had a bit of trouble with the two men the night before. "No gooders is what they were. We were looking to try to sell or trade some horses but looks like the lady isn't in too good of a condition to do much dickering." He told the alcalde that the man who got away was probably wounded as the boy and he had both fired at him as he ran out of the cantina.

The alcalde looked at the boy with eyes wide and said, "*Que* bueno, *hito*! Que bueno!" Turning to Palmer, he said, "I will ask some men to accompany me and we will search for this man. If I can be of a service to you and the boy, please, let me know."

Palmer and the boy, followed by the brown and white dog, went back outside and through the crowd of onlookers to untie their horses and mule. They then returned to the corrals and sheds where the ox drovers were and released their animals back into the corral. Palmer related their story to the drovers. As it was now about mid-afternoon, the drovers were eating out of a large pot of stew made from mutton, beans, and chili.

They invited Palmer and the boy to dine with them. They were almost through eating when a small carriage pulled up. The bartender from the cantina where the ruckus had been stepped down. Approaching them, the bartender addressed Palmer, "Señor, I am very sorry that this thing has happened to you and your son. The señora Barcelo would like to express her gratitude to you and the young man for what you have done."

Palmer replied, "Tell the lady that no thanks are necessary and all we need to do is sell some goddamn horses. As far as the man I killed, tell her that he was a no-good, son of a bitch anyway and I doubt that his own mother'll miss him. I know that the boy and I sure won't miss him."

The bartender asked, "Will you come with me to talk to the señora, por favor, señor."

Palmer said, "I doubt that she's going to be able to talk much about horse trading, so you go on back and tell her that Palmer Jackson and the boy wish her well." With a resigned look and a shrug of his shoulders, the bartender mounted the carriage and drove off.

After eating and asking the drovers to keep an eye on their livestock, Palmer and the boy walked back to the main street of the village in search of a store that sold clothes. As they walked along the street, Palmer spied a sign that was both in English and Spanish. It stated that it was St. Vrains General Store.

Palmer Jackson: Yankee Mountain Man

Upon entering the store, they noticed that there was a smattering of everything and they were immediately waited on by a young Mexican man who spoke English quite well. After asking what it was that they wanted, he proceeded to gather it up. He led the boy back to some shelves and proceeded to hold up wool shirts and britches to the young man until he was satisfied that he had found the right sizes. Then, he turned to Palmer and did the same. When he had gathered their clothes, Palmer asked the young man if there was a bathhouse or barbershop in the vicinity. He informed them that there was a barbershop where they could get a haircut or shave, if they could catch the barber sober. As far as a bath, the clerk told them that there was a lady who did laundry who might have a tub, but that she did most of her laundry in the river.

Palmer asked the clerk to include some homemade soap and to total their bill. The clerk smiled and folded his arms and told Palmer that Señora Barcelo had informed his boss, Señor St. Vrain, that if a man and boy with a brown and white dog were to come in that he was to let them have whatever they needed, and she would pay.

Looking around for the dog, Palmer noticed him laying by the door. He turned back to the clerk and he said, "Hell's sake, we didn't do nothing."

The clerk replied that from what the oxcart drovers had spread about the two of them and the dog, plus the two cantina incidents, that they were indeed celebrities.

Nodding thanks to the clerk, Palmer and the boy, followed by the dog, carried their package of clothes out and up the street.

Walking along they met a young Anglo man, who nodded and said, "Hello." Palmer inquired on the whereabouts of a barber. The young man replied that they had to backtrack about 10 or 12 buildings. The barber would be on the left and, by looking in the window, they could be sure they had him since he had no sign. Thanking him, they retraced their steps, stopping to peer in windows until they had indeed located the barbershop which appeared to also be his residence. Trying to open the door was futile as it was locked. Looking down at the boy and the dog, Palmer cursed, "Goddammit, boy, it don't look like we're going to be able to clean up."

As they were walking back down the street, they heard a clatter behind them and when they turned to see what the clatter was, they were being approached by the bartender driving the same carriage. Stopping the carriage before them, he said, "Pardon señor, but the señora Barcelo would very much like to thank you and your son. Would you please accompany me to the cantina? It would greatly please the señora and would remove me from much trouble with her."

Palmer looked at the boy and shrugged. "Hell, boy, we're not getting much done anyway. Might as well get done with this."

Stooping down, he picked the dog up and placed him in the back of the carriage where upon the dog attempted to jump out. Palmer held the dog in place and told the boy to get in with the dog. Once the boy had the dog, he gathered up their weapons and new clothes and climbed up by the bartender. The bartender started down the street but immediately reined the two mules pulling the carriage around and started back the way he had come.

Arriving at the cantina, he pulled the carriage around to the rear where a large corral and long, low adobe barn stood. As they got down from the carriage, a man came from the barn to unhook the mules. Palmer reached into the bed of the carriage and picked the brown and white dog up as the boy scrambled down. He handed their packages to the boy and then gathered up their firearms.

Following the bartender, they entered the back door of the cantina. As his eyes became accustomed to the shadowy interior, he noticed that the body was gone and someone had washed the blood from the floor. There appeared to be six men standing at the bar drinking. As he approached the bar, the boy and dog following, one of the men snickered and pointed at the boy and dog. "*Mi compadres*, the lady serves hitos and also perros."

Before Palmer could reply, one of the men at the bar said, "You better be careful, *cabrón*, these are the ones that everyone is talking about."

One of the other men approached Palmer and said, "Señor, please ignore Jamie because he is very drunk and knows nothing."

Palmer shrugged his shoulders and turned to the bartender. "Where is this lady?"

Before the bartender could reply, a low voice of a woman came from a corner of the cantina which was only lit by a single candle. "I am here, señor, and thank you for saying 'a lady.'"

Palmer approached the table and stood silently for a moment, studying the lady who sat at the table. Then, he said, "Lady, what is it that you need?"

She looked up at him and even in the dim light of the candle he could see the left side of her face was bruised and swollen.

CHAPTER SEVEN

The lady said, "Señor, I wish to thank you and your son as I am told that you prevented robbery and murder. Anything that I have is yours. What can I do to repay you?"

Palmer said, "Hell, lady, you don't owe us anything. I appreciate the clothes at St. Vrains, but it wasn't necessary. We're just looking to sell some Indian horses that we come by and maybe raise a stake. Right now, the boy and I only want to get a bath and maybe a haircut and a shave. We tried to find the barber, but someone told us that he was probably drunk and that we'd have to scrub in the river—which I'm not looking forward to as it's probably colder than a witch's backside."

"Señor, please, allow me to help. I can find the barber for you and your son, and then get you a bath. Please, sit down and have a drink as I have a room made ready and some water heated." She waved the bartender and a woman to her side and whispered in their ears. Then, they left and she turned to Palmer. "We have some tea with sugar for the boy and a bowl of water for the dog. What for you, señor?"

Palmer replied, "Damn, lady, that's a lot of trouble and we have got to get back down to where our possibles and livestock are, but that drink for me, tea for the boy, and whatever for the dog would surely be pleasing. But the other stuff, the young lad and I will make do. And again I thank you for the clothes."

"Señor, I have already sent for the barber and have someone heating bath water and Fernando, my bartender, who you have already met and most likely saved his life, has taken some men and a wagon to fetch your possibles and your livestock. Please, señor, allow me to make this small gesture to repay you for what you have done. Also, I would like to know the names of you and your son so that I may address you by your given names."

Laughing loudly, Palmer brought the boy forward and told Señora Barcelo, "Lady, this boy isn't my son, although, if he were I'd be mighty proud of him 'cause this lad has more grit than this whole room full of men. I regret to say that I don't know his given name, but according to a priest that doctored me a few weeks ago his surname is Chavez. You'd have to know the whole story to understand how this came about."

Just then two men entered through the front door dragging and almost carrying another.

Señora Barcelo said, "You must stay now, Señor No Name, for that is the barber that my men have returned with."

Shrugging his shoulders, Palmer turned towards the woman and said laughingly, "Hell, lady, after your going to all this trouble, it'd be a shame to leave. By the way, señora, my name is Palmer Jackson and the boy has only started speaking a few words the last day or two."

A woman approached the lady and whispered in her ear before hurrying off.

The lady nodded to Palmer and smiled, saying that perhaps he and the boy could stay long enough to relate their story to her. She then told Palmer that if he and the boy bath first, then they would try to sober the barber up enough to shear their hair.

Palmer Jackson: Yankee Mountain Man

Palmer told her that he would like to cut his hair and shave first since there were likely some visitors in his beard and his and the boy's hair and clothes.

She told him with another smile that she understood the problem, but the water was hot now. If the boy and he would go upstairs and bath, the barber should be sober enough to perform his job when they returned.

Palmer and the boy had to help the dog up the stairs. Upon reaching the room with the bathtub and water, Palmer told the boy, "Damn, boy! Look at that tub! Pure copper! Must have cost $30 or more." He told the young lad to strip down and get into the tub before he dug around in the package for the cake of yellow soap. The boy was still standing there and looking at the steaming tub when Palmer turned back around. The boy looked up at him with a bewildered expression. Palmer thought, *By hell, he don't know what's going on.*

There was a man who'd been standing there, waiting to bring more hot water if needed, but Palmer couldn't make him understand that he wanted him to ask the boy to undress and get into the tub and scrub himself. He gave up and slipped his worn boots off, removed his trousers and shirt, and stepped into the tub.

He then started scrubbing with the cake of soap. He ducked his head in the water and started trying to work up a lather in his hair and beard. He had a pretty good lather and decided to duck his head to rinse off the soap. Somehow, he got soap in his eye and could not get it rinsed out. The man with the hot water handed him a cloth to wipe his eyes. When he could see again, he could tell that the boy had been laughing at his antics in the tub. Palmer laughingly told him, "You little shithead, I'm going to get your skinny little ass in here and drown you."

The tub-man was smiling also. Palmer stood up in the big tub and scrubbed a lather up all over his body with the cake of soap. He then squatted down in the water and got most of the soap off, but the tub-man approached with a pitcher of water and indicated that Palmer should stand still and that he would pour water over him. The man raised the pitcher over Palmer's head and slowly poured its contents over him. Coming up out of the steaming water only to have the man pour cold water over him almost took his breath completely away, but he still had enough breath to utter, "Goddammit, that's damn cold."

The boy and the man laughed out loud at Palmer's actions.

Palmer stepped out of the tub and began drying off with the cloth the man had handed him. Palmer then located his new clothes and started to dress. Looking at the boy, he motioned for him to undress and get into the tub.

The tub-man stopped him, went to the door, and said something to two men with buckets. They came and began emptying the tub. When Palmer indicated that the boy could bathe in the same water, the man shrugged and continued emptying the great copper tub. When it was empty, and that took several trips, the same two started bringing hot water and filled the tub back up.

Reaching over and feeling the hot water, Palmer told the boy, "Hell, it's just about right to scald a chicken, so it should knock some of the dirt off of you."

Motioning for the boy to get undressed and get into the tub, he then began trying to locate his old clothes. Not finding them, he went to the door and hollered at the bartender. In a moment, he heard footsteps coming up the stairs.

The bartender stuck his head in the room and said, "*Si, señor*, you need something?"

Palmer said, "Yes, where're my clothes?"

The bartender said, "Señor, we were going to wash your clothes as they were very dirty, but they were also full of *piojos*—or how do you say?—greybacks. The señora told them to burn them. All of your other things are here." And he pointed to the corner of the room where the firearms, Palmer's powder horn, bullet pouch with his balls and patches, Green River knife, and small shoulder bag that he called his possibles bag were stacked. Also, on a small stool lay all of his money, several silver dollars and one $20 gold piece. His boots were missing also.

"Christ man, you didn't burn my boots did you," Palmer asked.

The man smiled and said, "Oh no, señor, but when the señora saw the boots, she sent them to be repaired. You will have them in the morning while in the meantime you must wear these." He produced a pair of wool socks and a pair of short boots. "Please, see if the boots will fit you."

Palmer sat down, put the socks on, and pulled on the boots. They fit just a little big, but he'd worn worse.

The man bobbed his head and left.

Palmer watched the boy scrubbing with the soap. He motioned for him to scrub his hair and face with the soap. After he got lathered up, he told him to stand and the tubman poured a pitcher of cold water over his head to remove the soap. It made the young lad squeal and dance around. Palmer shook his head and told him that he must be part girl as he himself had not squealed and danced around like that. Laughing and chuckling, he handed the boy a dry cloth and then sat down and watched as the boy dried off and started dressing. The new clothes were just a little big, but they still looked good on him. Palmer watched as the boy started to put on his old moccasins. He had wool socks that should help keep his feet warm until he could find a cobbler to make him some boots, in the meantime they'd have to make do.

After donning their clothes, they gathered their firearms and other items from the corner of the room and proceeded down the stairs to the barroom. Palmer did have to carry the dog down the stairs. However, he did notice that the dog seemed to be moving better than he had that morning. They found a table in the corner and stood their firearms and possibles against the wall behind the table.

The bartender came to their table immediately and hovered over them. "Señor, may I get you something to eat or perhaps a drink of some kind?"

Palmer told him, "Thanks, but we have to check our stock."

The bartender told him, "But, señor, your animals and belongings are all here. Please, go out to the corral and see them."

Tucking one of the pistols in his belt, Palmer started out the back door with the dog and boy following on his heels. When he reached the corral, he noticed that all five horses and the mule were in a portion of the corral and someone had thrown some hay in for them to feed on. Over in a corner of the compound, he noticed a privy. He'd had a pain in his gut for a bit so he walked over to the outhouse, went in, sat down, did his business, wiped on some pieces of rag that were in a bucket, and came out to face the boy and dog, who were sitting, watching him.

Palmer said, "Damn, boy, I think it's been two, hell, maybe three years since my big ass sat in a privy. We better be careful or we'll for sure be getting spoiled living like this."

Returning to the cantina, they found the lady sitting at the table where they had left her earlier. She said, "We have the barber somewhat sober, Señor Jackson, and, if you would like, he will shave your beard and cut your hair."

Palmer told her, "That sounds good to me but, please, call me Palmer and not Señor Jackson."

Palmer Jackson: Yankee Mountain Man

"Very well, Palmer. Perhaps the young man and the dog could stay with me while you visit the barber? Maybe he will tell me a story."

Palmer tried to reassure the boy that it would be all right to stay with the señora and talk to her, but when he started away the boy followed and the dog followed him.

Señora Barcelo smiled and said, "If you don't mind, I will follow along also and talk to the boy as the barber tends to you."

Palmer smiled at her and the boy and said, "I think that would be fine."

The woman pointed to a door across the room and followed Palmer and the boy with the dog. When Palmer opened the door, he noticed the man that had been half-dragged, half-carried in sitting down in a chair across the room. He immediately sprang up when he saw the lady behind Palmer, saying, "Pardon, señora, pardon." The woman shrugged and pointed to Palmer.

The barber pushed the chair to the center of the room and told Palmer, "Please, señor, sit down, please." He pulled two pairs of scissors from a bag and also a large calico cloth. After Palmer sat down, the barber wrapped the large cloth around Palmer's neck and shoulders. He then had Palmer lean back so that he could get at his beard. After taking as much beard as he could with the scissors, he then started on his hair. He worked a good 20 minutes on his hair, and the whole time the boy and the lady chattered back and forth in Spanish. Palmer had never heard the boy say over a dozen words the whole time they had been together. He was amazed that the boy seemed to be completely at ease with the woman.

The barber had a steaming kettle of water and soaked a large cloth in the hot water, then applied it to Palmer's face. The barber let the hot cloth stay on his face while he made a lather with a piece of scented soap. Then, taking a soft brush, he applied the warm lather to Palmer's face. Palmer lay there with his eyes closed, enjoying the warm lather spread over his face. He heard the barber strop his razor half a dozen times and then felt him approach. He heard a gun cock and opened his eyes to see the boy with a pistol pointed at the barber. The woman laid a restraining hand on the boy's arm and spoke to him in Spanish. The young boy uncocked his pistol, but kept watching the barber holding the razor next to Palmer's face.

The woman laughed a deep and hearty laugh and when she could breathe again, she told Palmer, "What I would give to have one so devoted and protective of me."

Palmer smiled at the boy and then nodded at the frightened barber to continue. The man continued shaving Palmer for about ten minutes and then got a warm wet cloth and wiped his face. He rinsed the cloth in warm water and then wrapped his face in it. As he was laying there in the luxury of the warm cloth, the lady was laughing again.

In a moment, she spoke to Palmer again. "This young man has only ever seen your face with a beard, now with your beard gone, he thinks that you are a stranger. That you will not know him."

Palmer took the cloth off and sat up. He looked at the boy and held his arms out. The boy looked at him for a long second before hesitantly coming to Palmer. As Palmer's arms enfolded the boy, he also felt the brown and white dog against his left leg. He glanced at the woman over the boy's head as he held him. He asked her, "What am I going to do with them and what're they going to do with an old fart like me."

She had tear-filled eyes as she replied, "You will live, Palmer Jackson, you will live."

Palmer Jackson: Yankee Mountain Man

Palmer gave the barber one of his silver dollars, but he would not take it.

The woman motioned for them to follow her, and then reentered the barroom. There was one man playing a *guitar* and another was playing a squeezebox. There was an older man singing what seemed to be a very sad song. They went back to their table and Palmer and the boy sat down. Señora Barcelo told them to wait. She went to the bar and brought back two hot mugs of tea and a bowl of sugar. She then returned to the bar and came back with two more glasses and a bottle of rum. She put a large pinch of sugar in the boy's tea mug and also in each glass, then filled the glasses half full of rum, added dry spice powder, and then poured the other cup of hot tea into both glasses. Pushing one to Palmer, she clicked her glass against Palmer's and then the boy's. Raising her glass, she told them, "*Salud*, señors, salud."

Palmer responded with a "Salud" and then looked at the boy and winked.

The boy picked his cup up and said a small "Salud."

The woman asked if they were hungry. Palmer told her that he was sure they could eat, if it wouldn't put her out. She smiled, went to the bar, and spoke to the bartender who went out the back door. He returned, smiled, and nodded at the woman.

She sat down at the table with Palmer and the boy and told Palmer that the boy had told her an amazing story about how they had met and their life had progressed. She wanted Palmer to tell her about rescuing the boy and his mother, but Palmer told her that all he could remember were bits and pieces of the time because he'd been laid up for four or five weeks due to getting hurt. All he knew was what the priest at the village of San Pedro had told him. She told Palmer that the boy had hesitantly told her of how the Indians had caught his father at the edge of the woods. He and his mother heard his father screaming and they'd run to the back of the house and climbed into a small hole that his father had dug next to the house. They'd pulled boards and brush to cover it up. His mother and him had lain there all night long listening to his father groan and cry out as the Indians tortured him.

The following morning had been when Palmer had drug his mother and him from the hole and they made a mad dash for the village. He had told her about the mule falling and breaking his mother's neck. How Palmer had killed the other mule for a breastwork and how they fought the Indians until the villagers showed up and drove the surviving Indians away. How one had hit him on the left arm with a club and how Palmer had been very sick for a long time.

Palmer told her that the old woman and the boy had saved his arm when everyone else wanted to cut it off. How the boy had taken care of him the whole time that he had been down. About how he dimly remembered the boy holding his pistol and keeping away a man with a knife and saw. How the old lady had laughed at him and gave him the drug to go to sleep.

He said, "It's very patchy, but I think the old lady and the boy saved my life. Then, I went off and left him with the priest, but he followed me with four horses and the brown and white dog, and I finally gave up and partnered up with him and I haven't regretted a damn bit of it. He's not very big but him and that damn dog damn sure pack their own weight. As the goddamn boat men say, 'he'll do to ride the river with.'"

Just then an older lady entered the room carrying a tray with bread, meat, rice, and beans. Palmer and the boy started eating and the woman got up. She told Palmer that she had customers and that she must take care of them. As she left, she told him that the boy's name was Andres Chavez. He had told her that now that he knew Palmer's name he'd like to be called Andres Jackson instead of Chavez.

As Palmer and the young man ate, he noticed that Señora Barcelo was dealing cards at a table to five men with others looking on. When he was finished eating, the older woman returned to the table with a tea pot. Palmer told her, "Thank you, but no." He said that the boy and him must be going.

A look of alarm crossed her face and she told Palmer, "No, señor, no, you must stay tonight. The señora has readied a room for you and your son. If you leave, she will be very upset and angry at me and my husband for letting you go. My husband is Fernando. He is the bartender here and he has told me how you have saved the señora's and his life. You will come with me, please."

Palmer looked over at the boy who was getting very sleepy-eyed and thought, *What the hell. I haven't slept in a bed in years, maybe I forgot how.*

With that, he gathered the boy and the dog up and, carrying all of their gear and firearms, followed the woman down a long hallway and by a large room with a large fireplace that was producing some welcome heat. A little further down the hallway, the woman stopped and opened a door. Telling Palmer and the boy to wait a moment, she went to the fireplace room and then returned with two lit candles and entered the bedroom. Placing the candles in two different corners, she told them that she would call them for the morning meal. She then bid them good night.

Palmer told the boy that they needed to go outside and take a leak. He had decided earlier that the boy couldn't understand anything that he said, and so had decided that he was going to have to learn Spanish in order to communicate with him. Taking the dog with them, they walked down the hall to a door leading to the outside. They then wandered around looking for the privy in the dark which proved to be futile, so all three relieved themselves against fence posts at the corral.

Going back inside, Palmer wondered about the dog sleeping inside and crapping in the room. He undressed and nodded to the boy to do the same. He then blew the candles out, pulled the wool blankets back, laid down, and covered up. He felt the bed move as the boy climbed in and then a few moments later felt the bed move as the dog climbed in next to the boy. He lay there and thought, *Damn, Palmer, if things haven't turned around. I wonder what the hell can happen to surprise me now?* He rolled over and went to sleep with as good a feeling as he'd had in a long time.

CHAPTER EIGHT

Palmer Jackson woke up before daylight the next morning and lay in bed quietly thinking about how he had survived events for as long and as well as he had so far in his turbulent life.

He had been born Palmer Joseph Jackson in a small cabin not far from the sea shore on July 1, 1783 in Kittery, Maine. He was the fourth child to be born to a family of eventually seven people.

His mother, Josephine, passed away when Palmer was 12 years old. He could still remember the funeral. It was the middle of January and the wind was blowing snow and tree leaves everywhere. He had been sure that he was going to freeze to death before the preacher finished the service. He smiled as he remembered what his father had said after the service as the whole family crowded around their stove trying to warm back up. His father had said, "There is not a fart's worth of difference between a Baptist preacher or a Catholic priest but for the size of their mouths and neither one knows when to shut it up."

He had four brothers, three older and one younger. His father owned a small fishing boat and all of the boys worked the lines, nets, and the few lobster pots they had. It was a tough, demanding life and his father was a demanding man.

In 1798, when Palmer was 15 years old, a man came through the village of Kittery, Maine, who would change his life. The little man came into Kittery searching for a ship to take him home to France. He wanted to see his mother before she died, if she had not died already. He was dressed in leather leggings, wool shirt, wool cap, and Indian shoes called moccasins. He immediately drew a crowd at the tavern in the village and regaled everyone with tales of the Canadian wilderness. He also told stories about the great desert 600 miles to the west. He talked of rivers that you couldn't see across, giant bears, deer and elk. Wild turkeys by the hundreds. Catching fish in lakes and streams so thick with them that you could throw an un-baited hook in and snag them. Waterfalls so big that you could hear the roar of the falling water for miles. He also told of seeing shaggy, wild cows. He said that they were bison, but all of the voyagers called them shaggy cows. He told of one herd that he had seen that had stretched from horizon to horizon and beyond.

Palmer's dad had to threaten violence on his boys to get them away from the funny looking Frenchman. After getting them all home, he gathered them around him and said, "Boys, you have just been listening to a braggart, a liar, and a teller of fairy tales. The man has nothing! Does nothing! And is nothing! We have a trade, a livelihood, a home, and believe in God. That man has nothing but tall tales to be told to children."

Young Palmer Jackson stayed one more year on the fishing boat, because he never forgot the stories of the wilderness that the little French Voyager told. On a warm spring day in May, he told his father that he wanted to go West and see the world. His father roared at him that the world was there—not wandering in the wilderness. Nonetheless, within a fortnight, Palmer had gathered together gear for a journey that his dad warned that if savages didn't kill him, then starvation and the elements would.

He had started down a road that very few people would try. His first winter was in the wilderness that people called Minnesota and he very near froze to death and would have starved if a French trapper and his Sioux Indian wife had not found him and taken him in. The Frenchman was called Chouteau and he taught Palmer to trap beaver and mink. They lived in a dugout covered with poles, and then a layer of sod. They built a lean-to to flesh and stretch the animal hides. On nights when the Frenchman was restless or drunk, his woman called Kla would crawl under Palmer's robes and blankets. So, he survived his first year in the wilderness.

In the spring, Chouteau, Kla, and Palmer loaded some gear and all of the pelts into two birch bark canoes that Palmer, Chouteau, and Kla made themselves. Palmer had helped strip bark from birch trees under Kla's supervision while Chouteau made the frame from green saplings tied together with leather strings cut from green hides. After laying the bark on the framework, they would then tie it to the sapling frame with more leather string. After completely covering the framework with bark that had been closely fit and then lapped on one end, the stern end, they gathered pitch from the pine and fir trees. They then covered all of the joints with pitch in two different applications. Palmer had grown up around boats and was rather skeptical about the canoe's seaworthiness. The Frenchman just smiled and told him to just be careful where he put his "big foots."

They let the pitch on the canoes cure in the sun for about nine days and then Chouteau said, "We go." First, they lay some pelts, hair side up, in the canoes, the Frenchman explained that this would give the canoe more strength.

Then, they loaded the rest of the pelts so that the weight was distributed evenly throughout the length of the canoe. Next, they loaded their firearms, some supplies, and blankets, and then they pushed off.

The little Frenchman told Palmer that they were on the Thief River and that they'd be on it three days before they reached their destination, the Northwest Fur Company.

The journey was exciting but uneventful. They had to portage the canoes and pelts only once, but that was enough for Palmer. They had to make about four trips carrying the canoes and pelts around the rapids. Then they reloaded and continued on to the Northwest Fur Company. When they arrived at the fur company, they beached their canoes and unloaded. As they were unloading, a bearded man exited the stockade and approached them.

When the man got closer, he hollered, "Ho, Chouteau, I did not recognize you as you look so much older. You probably have very poor pelts this spring, huh, *mon amie*?"

The Frenchman replied that he was very disappointed that the Indians he had talked with last fall had lied to him. They had told him that the blind Scotsman who lied all the time and worked for the fur company had shit himself to death. "But I can see you are still walking, and just as blind."

The Scotsman told the whole party to come into the stockade and he would have his people carry the pelts to the stockade. Inside the stockade, there were several log structures. The largest served as a storehouse and store. It had a long bar with several rough tables and chairs in front. The Scotsman went behind the bar and returned to the tables with several tin cups and a jug of rum.

As the Scotsman poured 4 cups of rum, the Frenchman told him, "First, I show you my friend Mr. Palmer Jackson."

The trader stuck his hand out to Palmer and said, "By the Black Billy Hell, young man, you could not be in better company. My name is Roger MacElroy. Let me serve you a drink of rum."

The Frenchman spoke up, "MacElroy, we must count the pelts and fix the cost before we can drink."

MacElroy smiled at him and motioned them to follow him. They entered a room with two large doors opening on the river. His men were already carrying the pelts into the room. He picked up, felt, and blew on the pelts, checked for cuts and slashes from skinning, and finally turned to the Frenchman and asked how many.

Chouteau told him, "104 beaver, 4 Wolf, 22 mink."

The trader took a chalk and small slate and began to figure. He turned to the Frenchman and asked, "American or English gold."

The Frenchman shrugged his shoulders and said, "As long as it is gold."

The trader turned back and said, "$350, Frenchman."

The Frenchman fell on the floor and screamed, "You, thief." He then stood up and told Palmer, "This man is why this river is named the Thief River. We cannot take less than $600 American and we are being robbed at that."

The trader, with a grave look on his face, said, "We can probably go to $400 and only because you are early, and we like you."

The Frenchman replied, "You will say you like me, but you cheat me so bad that we may starve in the winter. We will have to take everything back." He started piling pelts in the center of the floor. He motioned for Palmer to help him. They had stacked about half of the pelts as the Scotsman busily worked the chalk on his slate board. He stopped scratching on the slate and looked at the Frenchman again. The Frenchman looked at him and said loudly, "What?"

The trader turned the slate so that Chouteau could see it and it had $450 on it. The Frenchman took the slate, wiped it clean with one hand, then wrote $475 on it. He handed it back to MacElroy who glanced at it and said, "And you can call me a thief."

The Frenchman told the trader, "We take $475 and we keep the wolf pelts."

The trader was silent for a moment and then said, "475 and we draw high card for the wolf pelts."

The Frenchman and the Scotsman shook hands and went back in the store.

Palmer followed and realized that he had witnessed a proper business deal. They all sat down and proceeded to have a drink of rum. The trader went behind the bar and returned with a deck of cards and a leather sack of coins. He said, "First off Frenchman, the wolf pelts." He began to shuffle the cards and then laid them on the table.

The Frenchman said, "No, no, we must have Palmer shuffle the cards."

Whereupon, Palmer replied that he did not know how to shuffle the cards and he had never seen playing cards before and had never gambled in his life.

Then MacElroy said, "Cut the cards, Frenchman, and then we will each draw a card."

The Frenchman cut the cards two times and then drew one. It was a six of hearts, he groaned as he lay it on the table. The trader was smiling as he drew his card but he cursed mightily when he looked at it. He had drawn a three of spades.

The Frenchman jumped up and hollered, "*Mon Deiu*, the wolf is mine."

The trader began counting gold coins from the bag. They appeared to be new and shiny and Palmer asked to see one. The trader handed one to Palmer who looked at it in amazement. It had a date of 1795 and, on the back, said the United States of America.

The trader looked at him and said, "'95 was the first year the gold coins were minted. Lots of traders prefer them to the pound or sovereign." He continued counting out the gold to the Frenchman. When he got to 47 he told the Frenchman that he would toss the 48th coin and whoever called the upside won the coin as half belonged to each.

With a nod, the Frenchman watched the trader flip the coin into the air and he called, "Eagle-side" before it landed on the table.

The trader bent over the coin and then shoved it across the table to the Frenchman who was chuckling loudly. "You see, MacElroy," he said, "the luck is kissing me today." He took another drink on his rum and looked at Palmer. He asked, "And what are you to do my friend."

Palmer told him that he would have to find a job as he had very little money and must earn some somehow. He then said that he could do almost anything and he thanked the Frenchman for allowing him to spend the winter with him and his woman. The woman Kla spoke in her native language to Chouteau who smiled and nodded. He told Palmer she had said that some of the pelts should be Palmer's and he said that he agreed. He then counted out seven gold coins and pushed them across the table to Palmer.

The trader reached into the Frenchman's pile of coins and took one more which he then tossed to Palmer. He told the Frenchman, "For the wolf pelts."

The Frenchman threw back his head and laughed uproariously. He then shouted loudly, "Let us drink some rum."

The next morning Palmer asked the Scotsman to show him some traps, some new clothes, and provisions for a trapping trip. The Frenchman invited him to return with his woman and him. Palmer thanked them and expressed his opinion that if Chouteau and his woman had not befriended him that he probably would not have survived his first year in the Minnesota wilderness. But now he wanted to go West and investigate all the stories that he had heard about the far land. He had turned 17 years old some time that year but did not know when as time always seemed to run together.

The woman, Maria Barcelo, had told Palmer and the boy that it was December 10, 1830.

Palmer lay there thinking of his travels and what his father and brothers would think, if they even thought of him as still being alive. He wondered the same about them. Thinking back about his father questioning the integrity of the little Frenchman and his grand tales, Palmer thought that he would dearly love to see his family sometime and tell them that he had found all of the little Frenchman's tales to be quite true and that some were lacking as he had found some that were far greater and grander than even the little Frenchman had described. He had found that it was a grand land, a great land, and that it could also be a dangerous and demanding land at times. He lay in the bed and recollected that he was going to be 48 years old when the month of July rolled around.

He felt the boy move in the bed and decided that he would get up and relieve his bladder. When he rolled out of the bed and opened the door, he realized that the dog was with him. He stepped out of the hall door and walked towards some trees. He then pissed at the base of a large willow tree and he also noticed that the brown and white dog had humped up to take a crap.

Palmer Jackson: Yankee Mountain Man

When they returned to the house, the dog walked beside him. When he stopped to open the door, the dog pushed against his leg and, when the door opened, the dog went directly to the room with the boy. When Palmer got there, he could see in the half-light the dog was laying by the boy. Again his thoughts went back to what he had told the woman about the boy and the dog pulling their own weight.

How would things be scouting around for trapping territory? Would they be able to survive a winter trapping in the deep snow? He knew the boy did not want to stay behind and he decided that, by hell, he wanted him and the dog along. They were all the family that each other had. The woman had told him that the boy thought that he was 12 years old now and Palmer figured that he was still good for a few more years himself.

What the hell, come daylight he would see about finding something to do until spring, and then the boy and him would try their hand at trapping. They needed to locate a good area as absent of Indians as possible.

CHAPTER NINE

At first daylight, Palmer was checking their livestock that were in Señora Barcelo's corrals. As he was throwing hay into them, he heard a noise and turned to find the boy and his dog coming out of the cantina's back door. He hollered a good morning to the boy and received a bob of the head and a small reply in return. Not understanding him, Palmer decided that he must learn Spanish or the boy must learn English.

After each of them had visited the privy and taken care of their morning pains, Palmer told the boy to follow and they returned to the cantina to find the bartender's wife starting a fire in her cook stove. When she spied them, she motioned for them to sit down at the kitchen table. She soon had a large kettle of water steaming and then threw in a handful of tea. She let it steep for a few moments before she poured them each a small pottery mug full and sat a bowl of honey next to them. Palmer and the boy each put a couple spoonful's of honey into their cups and began to sip.

She was soon heating a large pot of beans and a pot of stew of some kind that appeared to have a large quantity of red chili in it. These people usually consumed only two meals of food each day—one in the morning and the other at night.

The bartender came into the kitchen and greeted everyone heartily. He had been cleaning and straightening the cantina of debris and stuff from the day before. He got bowls and spoons for everyone, his wife also, and began filling them from the two steaming pots. He and his wife then sat down, and they all began to eat. They had flat pieces of bread that she had cooked on the stove top. Palmer was informed they were called tortillas.

Everyone but Palmer seemed to enjoy the breakfast; he thought it was liquid fire. Even the young lad consumed the food readily. The bartender chuckled at Palmer and told him that he would soon be accustomed to the taste of chili.

After breakfast, the two men smoked. Palmer smoked his pipe; the bartender smoked a cigarillo that he rolled in a corn-husk. Palmer asked the man if he knew of any work that could be had as his money was getting short. The bartender told him that he would ask some of their customers about work. He said that with winter coming work would be hard to find.

Palmer then asked the bartender to convey to the boy his wish that they learn to communicate with each other. The lad smiled at Palmer and said, "Como esta, *ustedes*, Señor Jackson?"

The bartender looked at Palmer and said, "Señor Jackson, the boy said hello to you."

Palmer replied to the boy, "Hello to you, Andrew."

The boy asked, "Andrew."

Palmer said, "That's pretty close, isn't it?"

The bartender said, "Andres, señor, Andres."

Palmer said, "We'll straighten the name out later. Let's try to teach each other our speech, both Spanish and English." He told the boy to come with him and they'd walk around town and see what kind of work they could come up with. Palmer knew that it was the month of December and the approximate day thanks to the señora. If he and the boy could make it until February and the snowfall was not too deep, they could start to trap some beaver and mink then.

Palmer had over a dozen traps in one of his panniers. He wanted to locate some castor to bait the traps with. He'd set the trap and then insert a stake next to the trap. He then squirted a small amount of the castor on the stake. A beaver would swim by, smell the odor, and go to the stake to investigate. Then, from the trapper's view, step into the trap, thereby tripping the trap. The trap would be attached to a slide which would then drag the beaver and trap to deeper water where the beaver would hopefully drown. Usually, if the slide did not work properly, the animal would either spin in the water and twist their leg off or, in some cases, chew it off. Therefore, it was important that the trap and the slide worked correctly, or you'd have nothing

Palmer and Andres wandered around town looking things over. They were both amazed and very cautious as there was a large number of Indians around the village. They returned to the cantina around noon and Palmer engaged the bartender in conversation about the number of Indians in the village of Taos. The bartender explained to them that the village of Taos was actually built around an Indian pueblo. Also, he told them that the Pueblo Indians were very good farmers and nothing like the marauding bands of Comanche, Apache, or Sioux Indians. Palmer told him that, in his experience, when Indians were around your hair sometimes loosened up and disappeared. Palmer said, "I just can't trust the redskin bastards."

The young boy also nodded and remarked, "Cabron *Indios*."

The bartender admonished the boy for saying that. "Señor Jackson and Andres, these are good people." The young boy spoke rapidly and loudly for a few moments. The bartender shook his head, looked at Palmer, and shrugged his shoulders.

Palmer told him that if he had gone through the same thing that Andres had gone through that he would likely feel the same way that the boy did.

There did not appear to be a large amount of snow on the ground for the month of December in the high mountains. Talking to the bartender and Mrs. Barcelo, they seemed to think that it was a normal winter.

The bartender had conveyed Palmer's desires of finding work to Mrs. Barcelo. She then approached Palmer with an invitation to work for her. At first, Palmer vehemently protested, said that he couldn't take advantage of her by working for her. She then made him a different offer. What if she staked him to a trapping trip and they would then split the profits of the venture? He responded that it sounded like a great deal but that he had to sound the boy out as now he considered him to be a partner. Smiling, Mrs. Barcelo said, "I will present the idea to the young man."

Palmer went in search of Andres, who at that time had been in the barn caring for their horses and mule. When he entered the barn, he heard children laughing and giggling and became aware of Andres talking and laughing with three other children, two young boys and a girl. What everyone was laughing about was Andres on the mule. He would reach back with his heels and flank the mule who would then lay his ears back and pitch a buck or two. The children would then erupt with laughter and the dog would then join in by barking.

Palmer stood there quietly chuckling and reminiscing about his own childhood. He also noticed that Andres smiled and directed most of his attention towards the young girl. Suddenly, the dog noticed Palmer and crawled through the corral fence and ran to his side. The children noticed

Palmer now and became quiet. He motioned for Andres to come with him and, with the dog and the young boy by his side, he reentered the back door of the cantina.

Mrs. Barcelo was still at the same table and beckoned them to approach and sit down. Palmer asked her to broach the subject of her staking the boy and him to a trapping expedition. She smiled and said that first they should have some tea and honey. After the bartender had brought three pottery mugs and a bowl of honey, she smiled at the boy and began speaking in Spanish to him. As she spoke, the boy's eyes widened and he turned and looked at Palmer. She continued to speak for some time but the boy never took his eyes off of Palmer. She paused and then asked Palmer if he wanted to communicate anything else to the boy.

Palmer looked at the boy as he spoke to Maria Barcelo. "I want to be able to talk and listen to him and I want him to be able to cipher and read. I can teach him some but not all so I could really use your help." He turned back to her and immediately noticed tears coursing down her cheeks.

She smiled at him and said, "You may be sure of that."

That evening, Palmer, Andres, and Mrs. Barcelo sat around one of her card tables and she explained that Palmer wanted Andres and him to be trapping by the middle of February. To do so, there would be language, writing, and arithmetic lessons every afternoon to help them understand each other. Also, Palmer and Andres would be helping with the care of her livestock until they left.

Early the next morning, Palmer and the boy where in the barn as they wanted to meet the man who worked for Mrs. Barcelo taking care of her stock. A little after sunrise, a man and two boys entered the barn and started to care for the animals. Palmer approached him and introduced himself and Andres. The man smiled and offered to shake hands with them. He could not speak English and Palmer could not speak Spanish.

Talking to Andres, who could not speak English either, he explained that he was aware that Mrs. Barcelo wanted them to help him and his two boys care for her livestock and the barn. Palmer and Andres spent the morning following the man around, trying to interpret his instructions that he gave to Andres who then bravely tried to relate them to Palmer. Palmer did find out that the man's name was Octavio Espinoza.

As they walked around the barn and corral, Andres would point to something and then speak its Spanish name. Palmer would then speak its name in English and then try to speak the Spanish name. He was the center of quite a bit of laughter over his attempts at Spanish pronunciation.

By late afternoon, Andres and Palmer had gained a fair knowledge of how Octavio wanted the barn and horses and a few head of cattle to be taken care of. At their supper meal, Mrs. Barcelo imparted to them that Octavio and his family took care of a small ranch along the river and below the village.

Palmer had been aware that Octavio's children were the same ones who had been playing in the barn with Andres. Palmer mentioned to Mrs. Barcelo how the children had been playing together, so she asked if he would object to the Espinoza children being part of the learning session. Palmer said that he could not see any reason for them not to attend with Andres and him.

While Palmer and Andres were conversing with Mrs. Barcelo, two men entered the cantina and came directly to their table. One of them had a sheaf of papers and the other carried a rifle. With a very official tone, they started conversing with Mrs. Barcelo. She sat and listened for a moment and then she started to respond. The longer she spoke the more strident and venomous her voice became. Andres became quite still, and Palmer noticed that the bartender was watching what was happening very closely. He also became aware of the bartender setting a muzzle loading shotgun on the bar. Aware that something of consequence was happening, he started to rise. Mrs. Barcelo placed her hand on his arm and told him to stay seated. After saying a few more words to the two men, she then pointed to the door and they stalked out of the cantina.

Turning to face Mrs. Barcelo, Palmer's face presented a look of complete bafflement. She made a gesture for him and Andres to wait a moment, and then she made her way to the bar and loudly told the bartender Fernando, "Mescal *y tequila, rapido.*" The bartender produced two bottles and two pottery mugs. She returned to the table and poured mescal into one and tequila into the other. Taking a drink of tequila and then washing it down with a drink of mescal, she then slid them across the table to Palmer. He took a good solid swallow of the tequila and completely lost his breath, tears streaming down his cheeks as he stood and shouted, "Goddamn, what the hell is this?"

Mrs. Barcelo let a smile crease her face and replied, "It is tequila. Please, Palmer, let me explain some things. The man that was just here is our alcalde, our man in charge of order. You must understand that there have been stories circulating about an Anglo in our midst. The alcalde is quite nervous as it has only been eight or nine years since our revolution for our independence from Spain. Many people died as we fought the Spanish for our own country. Therefore, please understand, people are very suspicious of strangers. My own husband perished in a fight at Veracruz.

I hope that the alcalde accepted what I told him, but I am sure stories have spread about you and the boy. We must start some new stories that are more favorable to you. Perhaps what I told the alcalde about you saving mine and Fernando's lives will spread some goodwill for you. Please, be aware that we suffered for many years at the hands of Spain and we sometimes fear strangers."

Palmer smiled at her and then looked at the boy. He said, "You know it's only been 50 or 60 years since we went through the same thing, only with the British, so I can understand why your people're wary of strangers." Palmer asked, "Does the boy realize what's happened and how it'll affect us."

Mrs. Barcelo replied, "We will talk about all of this."

Palmer said, "You know he needs to know his history."

Three days later and, an unbelievable amount of patience on Palmer's part, he was retaining a smattering of Spanish words. Andres was able to speak a few English phrases such as, "My dog is brown and white" or "My horse is faster than yours." Mrs. Barcelo taught mathematics in the classroom using a deck of cards. You could use them to add, subtract, multiply, or divide. Within a matter of two months all the children and Palmer were conversing somewhat in English and Spanish.

Mrs. Barcelo had informed Palmer that her name was actually Maria Gertrudis Barcelo, and that she thought the children had progressed to a high level of retention. That he was the one now slowing the progress of everyone.

He told her, "Maria, it's the middle of February and I think that Andres and I can start setting a trap or two. Perhaps we can pay you back for everything that you've done for us."

She smiled at him and said, "*De nada*, Señor Jackson, de nada. You and the young man not only saved Fernando and my lives but you have given me great pleasure in allowing me to give you a chance to learn my language and to be able to teach these young ones about preparing for the world, for life."

Palmer smiled and reminded her that she had put up with and boarded Andres and him for over two months.

Later that night, as Palmer lay in his bed thinking about Andres, who was staying with the Espinozas for the night, he realized he was missing both the boy and his dog. He hadn't thought of family in a long time and now realized that the boy had become that to him.

Sometime later, after he had gone to sleep, he awoke realizing that someone was in bed with him. With a start, he realized that the person was female and happened to be Maria Barcelo.

CHAPTER TEN

The next morning, upon waking up, he felt that he was entering a new phase in his life. Maria Barcelo was not just a woman. She was a woman that he cared about deeply. She was a handsome woman of middle age who had taken the time to care and share her life with the boy and him. He knew she was an attractive female but he never thought that she could have had this kind of feelings for an old, grizzled bastard like him.

Rising quietly and carefully so as not to wake the woman lying beside him, he began to dress. As he was putting on his boots, he heard her say, "Are you leaving today?"

He sat there not responding, and she raised up on her elbow and repeated, "Are you leaving today?"

He quietly replied, "You really make it difficult to go."

She smiled and said, "Perhaps you could return to bed for a short while?"

Afterward, Palmer saddled some horses and waited for the boy and his dog to appear. When they did, he then went into the cantina and told Fernando that the boy and him would probably be back in the next two or three days as they needed to search for sign of beaver and possibly mink.

Palmer and the boy rode north out of the village, the two of them riding and leading a pack horse. There was about a foot of snow with drifts 2 or 3 foot deep in spots. They had very little conversation other than just prior to leaving, that's when Palmer checked to make sure that Andres had charged his rifle and pistol and made sure that both he and the young man had their percussion caps on their guns. They followed a rough sort of cart track up the river called the *Rio Grande* by the local people. Palmer was told that Rio Grande meant "Big River."

Palmer pulled his horse up and dismounted. He told Andres to dismount and they would relieve their bladders. It was also an opportunity for Palmer to tell the boy about some big rivers that he had seen. Andres listened to Palmer for a moment or two and then asked if there were really rivers that were so wide that you could not see across them.

Palmer chuckled and replied to Andres, "Boy, you've got some adventures coming to you." Palmer then told Andres that they were looking for beaver sign. The beavers would be chewing on small trees, mostly aspen, willows, and cottonwood. Palmer and Andres found a small stream running into the river from the west. Palmer decided to ride up the small stream. He was in front on his horse, leading a pack horse, with Andres following behind on his saddled paint horse.

About 2 or 300 yards up the little stream, Palmer and the boy rode out into a small park. Immediately, Palmer could see beaver sign. Stopping his horse, he dismounted and began walking along the stream banks. Turning, he motioned for Andres to dismount and come over. After Andres got there, Palmer pointed to where the beavers had been working the aspen and the willows. He said, while pointing to the brush that had been chewed on, "Beaver."

Andres glanced at the bushes and small trees and then exclaimed excitedly, "Oh, beaver is *el castor, Tio*, el castor."

Palmer threw back his head and laughed and roared, "Waugh." Palmer said, "Hell, boy, beaver or el castor, we're going to trap hell out of them."

Palmer Jackson: Yankee Mountain Man

Palmer and Andres moved back three or 400 yards from the stream and unloaded their packhorse and then unsaddled their riding stock. Palmer staked the packhorse out on about a 30 foot rope that was attached to one of her front legs. Palmer explained to the boy that the old mare didn't have much power to pull on the stake rope with her front leg and that if they tied the rope around her neck and she wanted go that she could either choke herself to death or break her stake rope and be gone. Next, they hobbled their saddle stock by tying a front leg to a back leg on the same side. Palmer told Andres that this was called sideline hobbling. They then turned the horses loose and watched the spectacle as the horses learned about hobbles. Andres was very impressed that the hobbles worked so well. Palmer also tried to explain to the boy about the saddle horses being geldings and that they probably would never leave the packhorse even if they got loose as they wanted to be with the female all the time.

At the same time, he couldn't help remembering his time with Maria Barcelo the preceding night and that morning. Smiling, he told Andres, "Goddammit, boy, when a female grabs hold of you, you end up thinking of nothing else."

He couldn't tell the boy exactly how that Maria Barcelo had upset his feelings about things this morning, but she had damn sure upset the applecart. He had been thinking that the boy, his brown and white dog, and he wanted to start drifting back north, trapping as they went, but that damn woman had sure thrown a bucket of cold, snowy water on his plans. She had been damn near all that he'd thought about all day long. Shaking his head vigorously, hoping to clear it of her, he hollered at the boy and his dog who were messing around in the meadow, checking everything out.

They came trotting across the small park to him and he couldn't help but notice that the boy's attitude and even his personality had changed. He didn't have quiet, silent, pouting moods anymore. He now appeared to be a happy, playful, normal young boy of 12 or 13 years. Palmer knew that it had to have been devastating to have lost everything that he had known in one horrible, bloody day. Palmer could relate to the same thing since he'd almost lost his own life only to have been saved by the boy, the old lady, and the people of the village of San Pedro.

Palmer couldn't imagine the mental torture and anguish that the boy had endured—and yet he had stayed by Palmer's side the entire time that he had been unconscious and laid up like an invalid. Palmer could still remember what the priest had said about how the young lad had made everyone but the old bruja back off and leave him alone. Every time that his left arm hurt, which was every now and then, he was reminded that he still had it mainly because of a young boy and an old woman.

Going to their panniers, Palmer removed half a dozen traps and their ax. He told the young man and his dog to follow and to remember to carry his rifle and pistol as they walked back across the meadow to the stream. They might get lucky and get some game for dinner.

The first run, or beaver slide, that they came to Palmer decided to set a trap. First, he found a ten or twelve foot willow, and cut it off at the ground. Next, he cut about a six-foot piece of rope. Taking the rope, he tied it around a large rock that weighed about 20 pounds, and then tied the other end to the butt end of the willow they had cut. He then waded out into the stream after hollering, "Holy shit, that's cold." After going into the water about thigh-deep, he then dropped the rock into the deep water and waded back to the shore.

Andres had laughed loudly at him as he hollered and, if he didn't know better, that dog was laughing also, with his tongue hanging out and everything.

Palmer Jackson: Yankee Mountain Man

Telling Andres to bring him a trap, Palmer took it and threaded the chain onto the willow. In about 6 inches of water, he stopped and sprang the trap open and latched the pan trip. Placing the trap in the water in a relatively smooth stretch of gravel, he then went to the bank of the stream and had the boy help him cut some willow sprouts and a small aspen sapling. He took those back out to the trap and carefully stuck them into the gravel next to the trap. Palmer then went back to the streamside and lay several large rocks onto the other end of the willow stick. Walking back to the shore, he then turned around to survey his handiwork. As he was standing there, Andres walked up by his side and said, "Señor Palmer, me no savvy, no *comprender*."

Palmer immediately began trying to explain how the trap would work if a beaver stepped in it. First, he broke a small willow shoot and, taking his knife, he cut a piece of the bark and squatted down to explain to the boy how the three of them were going to catch a beaver. Pointing to the piece of bark, he told the boy, "Señor beaver likes to eat the soft inner bark of trees, especially small saplings." He switched to his limited Spanish saying, "Señor beaver *quetis* comer," showing the boy the inside of the soft bark.

Then, turning to the trap they had just set, he showed him the small pieces of branches next to the trap. "Hopefully," he said, "señor beaver will smell the fresh cut branches and when he comes out of the water, he'll then rear up on his hind legs and walk to them and attempt to grasp them with his front feet. Hopefully, he'll then step into the trap and the instant the trap closes on his leg he'll sense danger. He'll immediately attempt to go to safety, to deep water. The chain will slide along the willow to the rope and hit the rock. He can go no further and the end of the willow prevents him from sliding the trap back up to the shore. If everything goes according to plan, the beaver is caught in the deep water and drowns. Sometimes, if they can somehow gain enough air, they'll chew their leg off. If the trap is set in deep enough water, they'll drowned."

The young man appeared to be very skeptical of Palmer's explanation. Palmer chuckled and told the boy that dark was coming soon, so they needed to go on upstream and set more traps. He also cautioned the boy about allowing Chico into the water as they set traps because it was possible that he could step into one of their traps. They only succeeded in setting three additional traps by nightfall.

They returned to where they had left their critters and their equipment. Palmer told Andres to gather some firewood and that he would try to fix something to eat. While Andres was gathering wood, Palmer laid a piece of canvas on the ground, it was about 8' x 8', and then he laid three wool blankets down on the canvas. Next, he took another piece of canvas of about the same size and covered their blankets. As the evening appeared to be cold and dry, he didn't think that they would need to hang a canvas for protection against the weather. He noticed that Andres had brought in a pretty good supply of wood and was attempting to light the fire with Palmer's flint and steel. Palmer let him try for a couple of minutes and then he stopped him, saying, "Goddammit, boy, you're going to wear that goddamn piece of flint clear out."

Realizing that he might have sounded a little harsh, he gently said, "Andres, let me show you a little trick." He then picked up a piece of dry aspen that the boy had carried in and pulled some dry bark off it. The dry inner layer he then took and wadded and crinkled up into a brown ball. Then, laying the mass down on a piece of bark, he told the boy to strike the flint and steel and try to send a spark into the wadded-up mass. It took about three attempts before they had a coal. He then showed Andres how to gently blow on the coal until he had a tiny flame and to cautiously feed small dry twigs until he had established a small flame, constantly feeding larger dry twigs and branches into the flames until he had a substantial blaze.

Winking at the boy, he said, "Damn, boy, you're now the official fire starter." Palmer then gave the boy a small kettle and their teapot and asked him to go down to the creek and fill them. When he returned with the two pots, they nestled them all amongst the coals.

Going to their panniers, Palmer retrieved two small leather bags and one larger one. He came back to the fire with the three bags: one bag had dried tea, the other small bag contained sugar, and the larger one contained beans. Palmer put four handfuls of beans into the larger pot and told the boy, "There's our breakfast."

He then put a couple of good pinches of tea into the other kettle and set it on the fire, waiting for it to boil. When the tea started to boil, he pulled it off of the fire and added a good dollop of sugar, then let it steep and cool. Returning to the panniers, he came back with a large bag full of jerky, probably goat or deer. He then handed two large pieces to Andres, telling him to give one to Chico but to, by God, eat the other one himself. As they were eating, Palmer told Andres that tomorrow they were going to have to find a deer or some other small critter for them and Chico to eat.

They stayed around the fire drinking tea and poking sticks into the coals. After the tea was gone, Palmer and the boy took their boots and coats off to get ready for bed. Rolling their coats as pillows, they then lay on one wool blanket and covered up with the other two and the piece of canvas. When they lay down, they were soon joined by the brown and white dog. Palmer let out a large sigh and told the boy, "It's a goddamn good thing that I like that dog or we'd probably eat him."

The boy responded with a muffled sound that could have been a laugh as he said, "Bueno, bueno!"

The next morning, at first daylight, Palmer and the dog were up and checked their livestock. He came back to camp and stirred coals up in the fire. After adding twigs and bark, he soon had a crackling fire going. He looked over to their blankets and saw two brown eyes watching him and the dog. He picked up a piece of bark and threw it at the boy, telling him to get up and help with their breakfast.

After the boy got up and took care of his bodily functions, they set the bean-pot on the fire. Palmer then told Andres to fill the tea kettle and they'd try to rustle something up to eat in a little bit. Palmer had brought about two dozen biscuits that the bartender's wife had given to him. She had said she sent them so that Andres wouldn't starve. She'd also sent a handful of peppers. Digging a couple of tin bowls out of the panniers and finally locating a couple of spoons, Palmer dished a bowl of beans for each of them, and the young boy crushed a pepper into his beans.

Palmer watched and shook his head. "I'm going to try some, but that goddamn stuff eats me up." He then crushed a pepper into his bowl and took a bite. He could feel the burn start immediately after he chewed his first mouthful. Glancing over at Andres, he noticed a big grin on his face. Palmer told him, "If you laugh at me you little fart, I'm going to drown you."

The boy exploded with laughter and then sprang to his feet as Palmer made a grab for him and missed. As he backed away from Palmer, laughing as he did so, he told Palmer, "Maybe you are like the little girl."

With that Palmer got to his feet and gave chase. Chico the dog also gave chase, eventually getting in front of the boy and tripping him which allowed Palmer to catch him. Palmer picked him up and carried him towards the river. The boy was screaming and laughing and Chico was barking and jumping as Palmer held Andres above the icy water in the river. Palmer told him, "If you ever call me a little girl again, in the water you go."

When he sat the boy down, he noticed that the first trap that they had set at the edge of the park had been tripped. He pointed at it and said, "We got something, boy, let's finish our breakfast and check our traps."

They finished their beans and a couple of biscuits a piece, washed it down with some sweet tea, and then scraped their bowls out and rinsed them in the clear water of the stream. Palmer noticed that Chico ate all of the beans and pieces of left-over biscuit with gusto and then looked for more. Finished with their camp chores, Palmer and the boy ventured to the edge of the park where they had set their first trap.

Locating the end of the willow that they had tied their trap to, they then started pulling it into shore. As it got closer, they could see that something besides the big rock and the trap was coming in. They had caught a medium-sized beaver. When they had finally got everything onto dry land, Palmer laughed at Andres and Chico as both he and his dog were jumping and laughing and poking at the dead beaver with a stick.

Palmer calmed the boy down and then again showed him how the beaver had walked over to eat the tender willow and aspen shoots, then tripped the trap and swam towards the deep water and hopefully safety, but he had pulled the trap down the willow and onto the rope that was anchored by the large rock. Unable to swim further and unable to swim back to shallow water because he couldn't get the chain past the butt of the willow that the chain had slid down, the beaver then drowned.

Palmer and Andres then tipped the trap and removed the beaver. Palmer then had Andres cut some more willow and aspen shoots. While he was doing that, Palmer carried the large rock and rope back into the deep water. Taking the trap, he slipped the chain up the rope and onto the willow. He set the trap down in the shallow water about where they had set it before. Andres had by then cut around 10 or 15 aspen and willow branches and he waded into the cold water and helped Palmer bait the trap again.

Finished, Palmer and the boy hung the beaver up in a tree and then continued downstream to their next trap. Andres asked Palmer about skinning the beaver and Palmer told him that they would check all their traps first and then reset any that had been tripped. By midday, they had collected five beavers and reset all the traps that had been tripped.

They had to make two trips to carry all their beavers to the park. Palmer estimated that the critters they had caught weighted from 35 pounds up to about 60 pounds. He and the boy spent the rest of the day skinning beavers.

It had been a day of education for Andres. He had learned how to trap beaver and then how to skin them and to stretch their pelts. He found out that after he trapped one the real work started. He had to be very careful when skinning so as not to nick the hide because that reduced the value of the pelt and that caused Palmer to use some very colorful language. After skinning, he had to stretch the hide until it was dry.

Andres was amazed when Palmer and he cut willows about 8 to 10 feet in length and then bent them end to end to form a rough circle. Tying the ends together, they then would lay a pelt across the willow framework. Then, they tied the pelts to the frame. By the time they finished, all five pelts were drying and it was getting late.

That night, after the dark set in, Palmer sat smoking his pipe and conversing with Andres, trying to increase both of their understanding of each other's language and speech. Andres was becoming more relaxed and sociable with Palmer Jackson and in turn he was letting Andres and Chico's presence become sort of an everyday occurrence. Andres seemed to be enjoying learning from Palmer certain words and their meanings. The same for Palmer with Andres and the Spanish language.

They spent a total of nine days and eight nights before Palmer Jackson decided that their supplies were becoming skimpy. They decided they had probably better return to the village of Taos.

There was also a strange feeling, like emptiness, that seemed to point Palmer back to what had transpired between Maria Barcelo and him. He decided that the situation needed to be confronted.

CHAPTER ELEVEN

The ninth morning, Palmer spoke to Andres saying, "Let's saddle up and go back to town." Saying that certainly wasn't as easy as doing it.

Palmer and Andres got all their gear ready to load, but their horses weren't quite as ready as their riders to leave. It really wasn't a lot different than any other time—except that their horses had rested well and were not inclined to be saddled and loaded. Palmer again showed Andres how to tie a horse's leg so that he could saddle them and be able to mount. Their mounts weren't too bad but the Indian horse that they were packing succeeded in bucking the pack off two different times. The third time, Palmer had Andres get on his saddle horse and when he rode by Palmer, who was holding the halter rope of the packhorse, handed him the rope and told him to wrap the rope around his saddle horn at the same time Palmer jerked the rope off of the horse's hind leg. The horses took off. Hollering at Andres not to stop, Palmer then mounted his horse and thumped the gelding's ribs pretty hard in order to catch up with Andres. When he caught up with Andres and the boogery packhorse, Palmer hollered, "Keep the sons of bitches headed south, towards town, boy."

Andres grinned at Palmer and hollered, "WHOO HAUGH."

It took about 15 minutes before the horses settled down and lined out down the creek towards the river and Taos. Palmer had noticed that Andres had not panicked during the episode of loading the packhorse and, in fact, he had chuckled several times. Palmer wasn't sure if he had been chuckling at the horse's antics or Palmer's voracious use of the English language. Whatever the reason, they had gotten everything loaded on the jug-headed horse, even the fresh beaver hides, which was probably the reason that the critter had been so obstinate about being packed.

As they rode along, Palmer watched Andres talk to his dog and the horses. It brought a warm feeling all over his body. Palmer grinned at the boy with his dog and thought, *Goddamn, life ain't so bad.*

It took the rest of the day and into the night to reach their destination. When the lights of Taos came into sight, Palmer felt an anticipation that he had never felt anywhere or any time before. As they rode down the street, he thought, *Goddammit, man, that woman is going to have your old ass acting like a barn-soured old horse!*

When they turned into the barn behind Maria's cantina, they could tell something was out of whack. There were lanterns burning everywhere, even in the barn.

Palmer and Andres unloaded and unsaddled their horses before they entered the rear of the cantina. Palmer noticed right away that Fernando the bartender wasn't there, and that Octavio, Maria Barcelo's ranch hand was behind the bar. He heard a sharp intake of breath as they approached the bar and he wheeled in apprehension.

Sitting at a table was Mrs. Barcelo. She held her arm which had the hand swathed in white bandages.

"What the hell happened, Maria?" exploded from his lips.

Palmer Jackson: Yankee Mountain Man

Before she could reply, her body began to shudder and shake and tears coursed down her face. Palmer knelt by her chair and gently gripped her uninjured arm. Andres stood next to Palmer. She gripped Palmer's shirt with her good hand but she was sobbing so bad that she couldn't speak.

Octavio walked around the bar and then spoke from behind Palmer. "Señor Jackson, while you and Andres have been gone, evil things have happened here."

Palmer loudly said, "What the hell are you talking about, man?"

Octavio said, "Señor, let me explain what has happened and the problems that have occurred. Palmer, do you remember several months ago when you and your young man walked into Mrs. Barcelo's cantina and surprised a man threatening murder and worse to Fernando and Mrs. Barcelo?"

Palmer said, "Yes, man, goddammit, get on with it."

"Please, sir, give me a moment to explain," Octavio responded. "You and Andres saved Fernando and Mrs. Barcelo's life most probably. You and the boy shot and killed one of the murderers. You shot and wounded the other one. The men from the village searched for him, but he eluded them. Now, almost 3 months later, and while you and Andres have been gone, this man and two others returned and have wreaked havoc on this lady. They came yesterday morning when most people were still sleeping. They murdered Fernando and his wife and then they took Mrs. Barcelo and they brutalized her. They took her right hand and cut off two of her fingers. The man said that you had killed his brother and so he would claim two lives for one. Fernando and his wife for his brother. He said that he had lost a finger in the fight so he would take two of Mrs. Barcelo's fingers. He also said that he was not yet satisfied and that perhaps if you were not a little girl, his actual words were a little pussy, pardon me, Señora Barcelo, but that was his words. He said that he would wait for you in Bernalillo, below Santa Fe. His name is José Benavidez."

Palmer tried to stand, but Maria had a steel grip on him. Not wishing to hurt her, he squatted and looked into her eyes.

She voiced an appeal between sobs, "Please, wait."

Palmer attempted again to stand, but she held him down.

"Please," she said, "wait."

Octavio spoke, "Palmer Jackson, listen to Maria Barcelo, the alcalde took some men to try and stop José Benavides from fleeing, but it has been three days and they have not yet returned. We need to think this thing through."

Palmer looked at Octavio for a full minute and then turned back to Maria. He looked into her eyes and said, "He will pay, Maria, he will pay."

Maria, still sobbing, replied, "Please, wait 'til the alcalde and his men return."

Palmer squatted there for a moment, gazing up into her eyes, and then said, "You know, I don't know if any of my family back in Maine are still alive and so, if you're so inclined, I'd sure like to consider you and the boy as my kin. I know that I have no right, but it would surely please me if you could see it as such."

Maria Barcelo sobbed harder than ever and could do nothing but nod her head and squeeze Palmer's hand.

Andres couldn't understand everything that had been said, but Octavio translated for him and after Octavio was through, he walked forward and gripped Palmer's other hand and nodded his head. "Si, Palmer Jackson, *es* muy bueno. Gracias." As he finished speaking, Mrs. Barcelo motioned him forward and, releasing Palmer's hand, she encircled the boy's body with her good arm and, speaking in Spanish, told him that nothing would please her more than to have the two of them as family.

Octavio brought three small glasses of red wine, two glasses of sour mash whiskey, and a bottle of tequila. Octavio's wife and children came into the barroom carrying bowls of hot stew and stacks of tortillas. Maria invited everyone, including Octavio and his family, to sit and eat. There was very little conversation until everyone had finished their stew. Palmer took his pipe out and filled it with tobacco, he then passed his tobacco pouch to Octavio who proceeded to roll a cornhusk cigarillo and hand it to Maria. Octavio's wife brought a coal from the stove and Maria and Palmer lit their pipe and cigarillo.

Maria told Palmer, "I have not smoked for three days, thank you. Now, we must talk. I must apologize for my actions earlier tonight."

Palmer replied, "Maria, please, no apologies, you've been through hell and most people probably wouldn't have survived. I promise you that man who calls himself José Benavides will beg me for mercy before he dies."

Maria replied, "Palmer, you must not be rash in your actions, you must wait until the alcalde and the other men return, this animal is hoping that you will rush out with no thought and fall into a trap."

Palmer smiled and said, "I've been in traps before." Turning to Andres, he said, "Andres, why don't you take the other children out and show them what we brought back in the pack?"

The children were hesitant until Octavio told them all to take a lantern and go to the barn and check everything out. Andres walked around the table and squeezed the shoulders of first Palmer and then Maria. He then told the other three children to come with him.

After they left, Palmer took a large swallow of the sour mash whiskey and shuddered as it went down. He said, "I don't see that I can do anything other than find Benavides."

Octavio spoke, "He knows that you will come, and he will hide and try to kill you."

Palmer said, "I know that, but there're some things that you can't control. I'm worried about the boy. When I leave, he's going to follow, and I don't know how to stop him."

Maria said, "Palmer Jackson, you must understand that the young man is yours. I think that if something happened to you it would be more devastating to him than what has happened to his blood parents. And I think that if something happened to Andres that you would be devastated."

Palmer spoke, "But how can I keep him from going with me when I go after Benavides?"

Maria thought for a moment and then said, "Perhaps I can convince him to stay and help me, perhaps to protect me."

Palmer said, "That's a good idea. Can you cry again? That was convincing."

Maria Barcelo slammed her wineglass down on the table and shouted at Palmer, "Cabron *pendeho*, you think I was pretending? I don't pretend, cabron pendeho." She then jumped to her feet and rapidly walked out of the room with Octavio's wife following close behind.

Octavio told Palmer, "You must be careful when speaking to women, they have different thinking than us."

Palmer said, "What the hell? I just thought that she might help keep the kid out of danger. I didn't mean to make her mad."

Octavio told him that he probably should go and tell Maria that he had misspoke. Palmer said that he had only spoken about an idea to keep Andres from following him.

Octavio said, "Señor, I think that for the peace of this place that you should go and ask her to forgive you for your thoughts about her crying."

Palmer said, "What the hell for? All I did was mention that maybe if she cried again perhaps the boy would be impressed and stay here."

"Señor, I can tell that you are not—how do you say?—familiar with ladies' feelings and ideas. You will have to go and say 'forgive me for hurting your feelings,' then perhaps you can talk with her."

Palmer Jackson said loudly, "Goddamn, I like that lady—I just don't know what the hell I did wrong."

Octavio told him, "Señor, believe me, for ladies are—how do you say?—they are not like us. If you will go and find her and my wife and tell them that you feel that maybe you should not have said that she cry for show, I think that she will forgive you. Remember, the women do not think quite as you and I do. Go on and, if the children come back, I will detain them here for a time." He stood and then urged Palmer down the hall where the women had gone.

As Palmer walked down the hallway, he realized that he had spoken words that somehow had upset Maria, but he still didn't know how to solve the problem. He stopped before a door where he could hear the murmur of voices coming from the other side. Standing still for a moment, he finally summoned the will to knock on the door. As soon as he knocked, he heard Octavio's wife ask, "Who is there."

He identified himself, and there was a moment of silence. Then the door opened and a red-eyed Maria stood in the doorway. He stated, "Maria, I know that I've offended you and I'd like to tell you that I'm very sorry for that because I have great feelings for you."

She was suddenly sobbing again, tears streaming down her face.

With a complete look of confusion, he backed into the hallway. As he was backing into the hall, Octavio's wife squeezed past Maria, grabbed Palmer's hand, and proceeded to pull him into the room with Maria. She turned and walked into the hall, shutting the door. As she closed the door on the two, she spoke to Maria, "Que bueno, *hita*, que bueno."

Palmer stood watching Maria with a confused look on his face and simply didn't know what to do. Maria suddenly wrapped her arm around him and sobbed more than ever. It was several minutes before she stopped crying and sobbing.

Still holding on to Palmer with her good arm, she talked softly. "Palmer Jackson, it has been a long time since I have thought of a man as I think of you. I will not fight with you. I know that you will go after this Benavides animal, but please realize that I have lost one man and I do not wish to lose you after I have just found you. You must understand that the young man, Andres, has feelings for you also. You should be filled with pride at the feelings that he expresses for you."

Palmer replied that he felt the same way about the boy, he simply wanted him to be safe.

She nodded, said that she understood and that she wanted the same thing.

Palmer and Maria spent the entire night talking and becoming more familiar with one another. Maria told him that Andres talked about what Palmer and he had done as though it was something sacred. Palmer told her that he'd like to somehow have Andres stay safe with her.

She said that she would try to convince Andres that he needed to stay and help her while Palmer was gone. "But Palmer, I know that you are going to go after this animal and I really fear that he will trap you. Please understand, if you stay, we will survive."

"Maria, if I don't make him pay, he will come back and do something far worse."

She sobbed and nodded that she understood. She said, "Do you not understand that since you and Andres have come into my life that I don't want you to go and Andres would be devastated if something were to happen to you? You should see how he talks about you. He has elevated you to a high place. I know that you must do this, but you have only just come into this old lady's life and I am going to be very selfish with your presence."

After she had finished speaking, it was quite a few moments before Palmer could speak. He said, "Maria, I want you to know that an old, gray-bearded bastard like me doesn't know what to say to a woman like you. I want you to know that I'm not as good a man as you think I am. I've done lots of stuff that wouldn't pass the test for a good man."

She replied, "If you could only hear that young man describe who you are and what you have done for him. And I know what you did for Fernando and me."

Palmer replied, "Goddammit, woman, Fernando and his wife are dead, and you have a crippled hand. I should have killed that Benavides bastard when I first had the chance."

Maria said, "Palmer, if you and Andres had not come into the cantina on that day, I would already be dead."

Palmer said, "Hell, Maria, I've got to leave in the morning and try to find that scum."

Maria replied, "Palmer, if you must go, please first let us have one more night together."

Palmer said, "Woman, what about your hand?"

Maria smiled and said, "Palmer, it does not hurt too much."

CHAPTER TWELVE

In the cantina's barroom, Octavio and his wife listened to the quiet and smiled at each other.

Andres and the three other young people came back into the cantina laughing and chattering as young people do. Andres looked around with a perplexed look. He turned to Octavio and said, "Señor Espinoza, where?"

Octavio motioned for him to come closer and then he quietly told him that Señor Jackson and Señora Barcelo were spending some private time together and that Andres needed to spend the rest of the evening with his family.

All the young people chattered the night away about the beaver and mink pelts. Andres's dog, Chico, had an altercation with the Espinozas' dog, a black and white female who soundly whipped Chico, who was larger than she. Andres told everyone that he could not understand why.

Octavio chuckled and told him that as he got older he would come to understand this strange phenomenon.

When the sun came up, it found Palmer in the corral behind the cantina, catching his saddle horse and then a horse to pack. Within 30 to 40 minutes, he'd saddled his riding horse and thrown a pack on the other horse. As he was finishing, Andres came out of the cantina's backdoor and started to catch a horse for himself. Palmer told him to wait a moment and put his arm around him. He walked the boy back to the cantina where a bench stood.

Palmer sat down on the bench and motioned the boy to sit down with him. As the boy sat down, Palmer began talking, telling him that he needed him to help him with something important. He asked Andres if he trusted him, and the boy nodded that he did. Palmer told him, "I need you to stay and help Octavio and his wife take care of and protect Maria Barcelo."

Andres jumped to his feet saying, "You go?"

Palmer said, "Yes, I have to try to find Benavides before he comes back and hurts other people."

Andres turned back towards the corral. "I go with you."

Palmer stood and walked to him, saying, "Goddammit, Andres, I have to do this alone and I need you here."

"But, señor—" he began.

Palmer slashed his hand down, saying, "Boy, I can't have it."

At that time the back door of the cantina opened and Maria Barcelo emerged. She said, "Andres, please, will you and Palmer Jackson please sit down with me and talk?"

The boy and Palmer slowly turned, walked back to the bench, and sat down next to her. She began by making a statement that she thought that Andres and Palmer belonged to her, so she would like to interject her thoughts into this conversation. She told them that she was very worried about Palmer going after Benavides, but that she realized that something should be done and waved her bandaged hand in front of them both. "Fernando and his wife are gone. I am the only one left, so I think that I have some say in this matter. Andres, your friend and companion, Señor Jackson feels that he needs to retaliate against Benavides. He also thinks that Benavides could possibly circle around and attack us again. He and I would appreciate it very much if you and your dog, Chico, would stay for a few days while he is gone to provide me with some protection—at least until the alcalde and his men return, and perhaps you can help me around the barn."

With a downcast glance, Andres looked at Palmer and said quietly, "Si, señora."

She replied, "Gracias, Andres, gracias."

Palmer said, "Goddammit, boy, I don't have the grace of speaking words like Maria, but it would help a bunch if you can do this. I'll leave you one of the Harris rifles and a pistol. If that bastard, pardon the language, Maria, but if he shows up—you don't hesitate, you take him out. You know what to do. I know that Maria and I can depend on you to do what needs to be done."

The young man nodded and replied, "Si, señor, I can do it."

Palmer gripped Maria's good hand and said, "Thanks, I just can't talk like that."

Maria said, "Palmer, you must go but you also must come back, is that not so, Andres?"

Andres replied, "Si, señora, it must be that way. Señor Palmer Jackson, I will wait for you, but you must return."

Maria said, "That is correct, Palmer Jackson, you have entered our lives in such a way that we do not want you to leave us."

"I understand, Maria, and, believe me, I don't really want to leave, but I think this thing must be done. Andres, come and help me get everything ready." Palmer stood, reached down, and squeezed Maria Barcelo's shoulder. He said, "Thank you very much. I'm trying to learn about these things, and I hope that I'm not too old and gray to learn."

She said, "Palmer Jackson, you are not too old and gray for this young man and me. Just come back."

Andres and Palmer went to the corral and unhitched the two readied horses. Palmer then swung up into the saddle and gathered the reins in one hand and the lead rope of the packhorse in the other. He looked down at the boy and said, "Take care of things, boy, and keep your eyes peeled."

"Si, señor," said Andres and he backed a few steps away. "*Adios*, señor, adios."

As the horses turned into the street, the boy hollered, "*Ten cuidado*, señor, ten cuidado."

When Palmer looked back, he saw Maria standing, watching with Andres next to her, her good arm around the boy's shoulders.

Palmer had never been south of Santa Fe, which was filled with people from all over, but Benavides had said to come to Bernalillo which Octavio said was about 60 miles south of Santa Fe. Palmer only made about 15 miles the remainder of the first day and spent the night along the Rio Grande.

He was up with the sun and spent about an hour fixing and eating a morning meal of sorts: tortillas, some jerky, and tea. He then cleaned up and caught the horses up. By the time he had saddled his riding horse and packed the other horse with his possibles, the sun was up pretty good. He started south again, towards the town of Santa Fe. Octavio had told him that even if he made pretty good time, it would probably take two full days, possibly three, more to get from Santa Fe to Bernalillo.

Palmer was going to try to make Santa Fe in two days, but he didn't think that it was possible now that he had gotten a slow start the day before. He kept his saddle horse in a brisk trot with the packhorse's halter rope wrapped around the horn of his saddle. He was crossing a small stream that ran into the river when he decided to stop and let the horses drink for a moment or two—but then he saw a flicker of movement coming towards him along the trail. His Harris rifle was hanging by a leather thong from the saddle horn. He immediately pulled the Harris off of the horn and made sure the percussion cap was in place and his powder flask hung from his shoulder with his pouch full of balls and other items.

He spurred his saddle horse off of the trail, pulling the packhorse with him. Dismounting and tying up the two horses, he then found a defensible spot next to the trail. It was but a short time when a group of men came into view and Palmer recognized the alcalde and three other men on horses coming up the trail towards him. When they got closer, he stepped out into the muddy cart track and raised his hand in greeting.

The men pulled up a short distance down the trail and Palmer hollered at the alcalde, identifying himself. The group came forward and greeted Palmer, asking what he was doing here. Palmer told them that he was looking for Benavides and asked them if they had had any luck searching for him. The alcalde motioned for the men to dismount, which they did. The alcalde asked, "Señor Jackson, what are you doing here by yourself."

Palmer replied that he was searching for Benavides and that he understood that they were doing the same and perhaps that they had gotten lucky and got the no-good, son of a bitch.

The alcalde spoke, "Ahh, señor, we have not even seen him or talked with anyone that has. We went about a day and a half below Santa Fe to the Indian pueblo of Santa

Domingo. We spent the night there and spoke to the priest, a father Sanchez. He asked the Indians to ask about the killer Benavides, but no one had seen him."

Palmer told the alcalde that he was going to go on as he understood that Bernalillo was about two or three days below Santa Fe.

The alcalde nodded his head and said that it was so. The alcalde told Palmer, "Señor, we must return as we have families that we must take care of."

Palmer said that he completely understood and thanked the four men profusely. He then explained the situation with Maria Barcelo and young Andres.

The alcalde nodded his head and said, "I understand the situation and I will try to calm them down when I return." He then spoke about Maria and Andres. He told Palmer that it had been some time since he had seen the lady smile and, he added, that since Palmer and Andres had entered Maria's life she was a different woman.

Palmer told the alcalde and his men that he was going on as Benavides had said that he would wait in the town of Bernalillo.

The alcalde told Palmer that he wished him good luck in his search, but that he must be very careful as Benavides and his men were very nasty characters, very untrustworthy.

Palmer told the men that he had been associated with this kind of man since he had left Maine as a young lad. "Please tell Maria and the boy that I'm going on to Bernalillo and I'll be careful."

The alcalde and his men promised to pass on his message.

Palmer again told the men that he really appreciated what they had done for Maria, Fernando, and his wife.

The alcalde replied, "Señor Jackson, it is my job to try and keep the people in the village of Taos safe. They appointed me as alcalde. I am very sorry that I have failed in this particular endeavor."

Palmer said, "Mister, you tried, and the people'll appreciate it. I know that, I surely do." With that Palmer mounted up and headed on south towards Santa Fe, and the alcalde and the other three men started back towards Taos.

Palmer had to spend one more night out and at noon of the next day reached Santa Fe. He found a livery where he could stable his horses and sleep in the barn. He settled his livestock and then went downtown where the cantinas were. He hunted for the most rundown-looking cantina as he was pretty sure Benavides and his kin wouldn't want to stand out in a crowd. They'd prefer to hide amongst their own kind. And if he could dig up where he should be meeting Benavides instead of Bernalillo and keep from walking into a trap, well, he'd be mighty pleased.

Palmer cradled his Harris rifle in his arms and stuck the pistol in his belt. He caused some conversations to end as he'd walk in, stand silently near the door, and look all around the cantina. He remembered Benavides as being shorter than normal with black hair and a beard. He also had ears that stuck out from his head more than usual.

By dark, Palmer had visited six different dives and had gone into one that appeared to be a little cleaner than the others and asked for a bowl of beans and chili. He was eating at the bar and casually asked the barman if he knew of a José Benavides. Before the bartender could respond, a man behind Palmer jumped up so suddenly that the table he was sitting at was up ended. Palmer turned swiftly, and that probably saved his life, as the man that had jumped up fired a pistol at exactly where Palmer had been sitting. Realizing he had missed, the man started to run towards the door. Palmer jerked his pistol from his belt and fired at the fleeing man as he jerked the door open. After he went through the door, the unknown gunman disappeared in the twilight. Grabbing his Harris rifle, Palmer ran through the door and glanced both ways, but he couldn't see anyone.

CHAPTER THIRTEEN

It was almost completely dark, and Palmer thought that the sensible thing to do was go back into the cantina, question some people, and then wait 'til morning to pursue the shooter. All talk stopped when he reentered the cantina. He walked over to the bar and asked the barman if he knew the man that had shot at him. The barman replied that he had seen the man on several occasions but didn't know his name.

An older man spoke up hesitantly, saying that perhaps he could help. He walked up to Palmer and introduced himself as Joquine Peralta. He told Palmer the man that he had shot at had a family by the name of Garcia and that most of this family was, "No bueno *por cagada*." Not understanding what the man had said Palmer turned towards the barman who told him that the older man had said the man that ran was "no good for shit."

Palmer said, "But I'd asked about a man called José Benavides."

The old man then told Palmer that this Garcia was related to Benavides through the mother who was a Benavides.

Palmer said, "Maybe cousins?"

The old man nodded his head in the affirmative.

Palmer immediately thought, *I bet that bastard was one of them. Probably all three were related.* Now he had somewhere to go and something to go on. He walked to the far end of the bar and tried to finish his bowl of beans and chili. The food was spicy enough that he asked the barman for a glass of beer. When the barman set a pottery mug of frothy beer in front of him, he asked what he owed for the meal and the mug of beer.

The bartender threw his arm up in a vehement gesture and replied, "Señor, please a man should shoot you and still you offer to pay, not this day, señor, but I thank you."

Palmer told the barman that perhaps he could buy Señor Peralta a drink.

Joquine Peralta stood up and came to the bar saying, "Señor, I thank you, but it is not necessary."

Palmer looked at him and said, "Mr. Peralta, I'd like to ask you about this Garcia man, and I'd consider it an honor to have you drink with me."

Joquine Peralta bobbed his head in the affirmative and told the barman, "Mescal, por favor."

Palmer talked to Señor Peralta for probably one hour and learned that Garcia lived below the Santa Domingo Indian pueblo, down on the river someplace. Also, he found that there were several families, Garcias and Benavides in a little community called Peña Blanca. Señor Peralta cautioned Palmer about going into the small village and asking about Garcia and Benavides as the village was almost entirely related to one another. He asked the elderly man for directions and was told how far down the river the community of Peña Blanca was.

"I can tell you," Señor Peralta said, "the Garcias and Benavides were like cagada, señor, the cagada."

Finishing their drinks, Palmer bid Señor Peralta and the bartender good night as he was wanting to get an early start in the morning. He walked back to the stable where his livestock were and found that the liberty man had left a lighted lantern hanging on the door. As he entered the stable, he was somewhat startled when a brown and white form flashed towards him. Palmer hollered, "Goddammit, boy, what in hell are you doing here?"

The brown and white flash was Andres's dog, Chico. Andres shuffled slowly out of an empty stall and slowly raised his head to meet Palmer's gaze.

Palmer again said, "Boy, what the hell are you doing here? I asked you to stay and take care of Maria Barcelo."

Andres replied quietly, "Señor, when the alcalde and his men returned, he said that he could protect Señora Barcelo, so I thought that perhaps Chico and I could help you find this Benavides. Then, we could all go home."

Palmer had to swallow hard to keep from cussing, but when the boy mentioned going home it changed things as it had been a hell of a bunch of years since anyone had associated the word home with Palmer Jackson. He turned about and walked through the door and back outside. Andres and Chico followed, and Palmer was silent for a moment or two and then asked, "How in the goddamn hell did you find me, boy?"

Andres hesitantly replied that he had checked corrals along the street and that his horses had actually recognized Palmer's horses and nickered at them. Then he and Chico had recognized Palmer's horses and had settled down in the barn to wait for his return.

Palmer said, "Goddammit, boy, what's done is done and I've found out some stuff about this Benavides. But first, I need to ask if you've had anything to eat for supper."

Andres was very hesitant in saying no, that he was not hungry.

Palmer then asked him if he had taken care of his livestock, and the boy replied that the livery man had let him put his horses in with Palmer's.

Palmer then told him to follow him back up the street. They reached the cantina that he had just left. As they entered the cantina, they both carried a Harris rifle with a pistol stuck in their belts. The bartender greeted Palmer with raised eyes and motioned to Andres.

Palmer said, "He's with me and I think he's hungry. Also, the dog's done many things for me. So, it'd be greatly appreciated if you could find enough food for the young boy and his dog. Someday, if you have enough time, I'll tell you their story, but for right now I'd appreciate if you could just get them some food."

The bartender smiled and said, "Señor, you surprise me every time you come in. They will be fed."

When they sat down, Señor Peralta came over and sat down with them and began petting Chico.

Palmer said, "Señor Peralta, this young feller is Andres and this is his dog Chico, and they kind of belong to me." He gestured to the two. "Andres, Señor Peralta told me where he thought that Benavides could be staying. Maybe you can ask him about where he thinks we should go." He waved at the old man. "Señor, would you care for another drink?"

"Si, si, *muchas* gracias." The old man then started asking Andres some things in Spanish.

Andres looked questioningly at Palmer. Palmer shrugged and told Andres to talk to Señor Peralta as he'd probably learn something to help them. It probably took a quarter of an hour for Andres's food to arrive, and the cook also brought a large bowl of food scraps for the dog. One of the other patrons laughed and pointed at the boy and the dog, whereupon, Señor Peralta immediately turned around and castigated the man who said something else when Palmer suddenly stood up. Before Palmer could say anything, the bartender loudly and vehemently told the talker to leave or shut up.

Palmer Jackson: Yankee Mountain Man

There was a strained silence for a few moments and then Señor Peralta spoke loudly and rapidly for about one half of a minute and then there was silence again.

The man that had laughed and pointed came to the table and grasped Andres's shoulder and squeezed it saying, "I am sorry, mi hito. I did not understand." He then turned to Palmer saying, "Pardon, señor, I did not realize that your son had traveled so far without you. You must forgive me as the mescal sometimes make me into a big *pendejo*."

Palmer waved him away and waited for Andres to finish his supper. He also thanked Señor Peralta for his help. When the boy was through eating, they went back to the livery stable to spend the night. They found a clean stall and spread some fresh hay to spread their blankets on. The two then went out into the corrals and relieved their bladders. Coming back into the barn, they removed their gear and lay down on the blankets and hay.

Palmer blew the lantern out and lay there for a moment and then asked Andres about Maria Barcelo and what she had thought of Andres coming after him. Andres slowly and quietly replied to his question. He said that Mrs. Barcelo was very upset at his leaving but he had told her that the alcalde had agreed to watch over her and that Octavio had also said that he would keep an eye on her.

Palmer said, "So, boy, you just rode off and they didn't try to stop you at all?"

Andres was quiet for a time and then told Palmer that there had been some opposition from Mrs. Barcelo and Octavio so he had been forced to leave in the middle of the night. He said that he had told Octavio's children to relay the message to both Octavio and Señora Barcelo that his only reason for leaving was his concern for Palmer's safety.

Palmer lay there a few moments silently thinking, *How in the goddamn hell can I fight that reasoning, much as I want to?* He finally spoke, saying, "Dammit, boy, that lady and Octavio really worry about you and me, but no matter, we have got to go on and take care of Benavides. Now, let's get some rest and see what the morning brings." It was only a few moments when he heard a rustle and realized that Chico had just bedded down with them. Palmer lay there thinking, *Goddammit, how in the hell can I holler at these two when I probably would have done the same thing if the tables had been reversed?*

The next morning, at first daylight, they were awakened by a rooster crowing and shortly after that the man who owned the stables came in and started feeding the animals. Palmer raised up on an elbow and voiced a good morning greeting to him and received one in return. Andres and Chico lay huddled under their blanket in the hay.

Palmer said, "Boy, we better get up and try to rustle us something to eat."

They got up, rolled their blankets, and put them with their riding gear. Walking around the back of the corrals, they located a privy and relieved themselves. They then found a large stock tank and washed the sleep off of them. Palmer and Andres took turns pumping fresh water on each other to rinse the tank water off.

Palmer and Andres, followed by the brown and white dog, ventured out onto the main street in search of food. Two or three streets down they could smell food being cooked and simply followed their noses to a small building with a sign in front that Palmer couldn't read but that Andres said was an eating establishment. The sign said *"café."* The two entered after Andres made Chico lay down outside because Palmer had told him that not all business places liked dogs coming into them. They entered and were greeted by some very welcome aromas. A very large woman greeted them and pointed to a table and asked them if they would care for some tea. Palmer said that he would, but he didn't know what Andres would drink. Andres told the lady that he would like some hot tea, if that would be okay.

The lady smiled at him and said, "Yes." She then said that her breakfast consisted of fried eggs, rice, beans, and steak for 25 *centavos*. Palmer smiled at her and then told her to fix up two of them as the boy and him were mighty hungry.

They were the only customers in the café and, as they waited for their food, the lady asked where they were from. Palmer responded saying that at this time they were from the village of Taos. She smiled and asked if perhaps they knew a lady by the name of Maria Barcelo. Palmer and the boy looked at each other and smiled.

Andres looked shyly at Palmer, grinned, and nodded, and then to the lady replied, "Si, señora."

She smiled and asked if perhaps they were the ones who, with a brown and white dog, had caused lots of talk in Taos.

Palmer replied, "Lady, I don't know if we caused talk, but we know the lady Barcelo and are sure beholden to her for the many things that she has done for the two of us."

Andres said, "Señor Palmer, but Chico too."

Palmer threw back his head and laughed causing the dog to bark at the door where he was waiting.

The lady smiled and went to the door and said, "Your name is Chico, so you may come in my kitchen."

The dog went across the floor and lay down between Palmer and Andres.

The lady came back into the kitchen and stood looking at the two of them with the dog laying between them. She said, "Perhaps you are wondering how I came to know of you three. About three weeks ago, I received a letter from my sister in Taos who happens to be Maria Barcelo. She sent me a very interesting letter telling about your adventures and describing what you were trying to do by forming a partnership with her. What brings you two with your Chico to Santa Fe?"

The food was hot and ready, so she asked them to wait until after she had served them to tell their story. As soon as the food was on the table and after he'd eaten a few bites, Palmer related their reasons for being in Santa Fe. When he had brought her up to date, she slapped the table and exclaimed that she had heard of this Benavides but did not know where he lived.

Palmer told her that Señor Peralta had told him that Benavides was related to a Garcia who had shot at him. Mr. Peralta also thought that Garcia and maybe Benavides came from Peña Blanca.

The lady said, "If that is so, señor, Peña Blanca is about two and a half days ride down the river." She added, "This Benavides is a man of low character. He has committed several—how do you say?—atrocities. I think that if you and your son had not interfered the first time my sister would probably be dead. You must be very careful as the Benavides and the Garcias are very numerous from Santa Fe South."

"What is your name, señora?" asked Palmer.

She replied, "My name is Viola Silva and if I can help you to help my sister, please, let me know."

Palmer and Andres stood up and tried to pay for their breakfast, but Viola Silva became very animated about it, saying, "You are like family so you must realize family does not do things like that. Please, you must understand about the Benavides and Garcias. You must be very careful because they are numerous like the hair on a cat's back."

Palmer thanked Viola Silva for the meal and more so for the information concerning the Benavides and Garcia clans. Palmer and Andres returned to the livery and settled their account. After they had saddled their horses and packed their packhorse, Palmer asked the livery man for directions to Peña Blanca.

The livery man complied by telling them that it was about two days ride south along the river. Thanking him, they mounted up, the little Indian horse they were packing followed their saddle horses without having to be led, and they started south, downriver.

CHAPTER FOURTEEN

Palmer figured that they made about 20 miles the first day before they made camp. They found a small clearing along the river that was surrounded by cottonwood trees with willows growing between. Palmer and the boy picketed two of their horses and hobbled the other one, allowing it to graze. They would change the horses after a few hours and allow the other two to graze.

It wasn't that chilly, but Palmer went ahead and made a small fire anyway to heat some water for tea. The river was rising as the spring runoff was in progress and the water was very muddy. Palmer showed Andres how to find a small depression along the riverbank and then take a stick and dig down about 1 foot in the wet sand and in a very short time it would fill with clear, drinkable water.

Their supper consisted of tortillas, jerky, and tea. Andres made sure that Chico received a couple pieces of jerky and some of his tortilla. Palmer watched and tried not to let the boy see him smile as he watched the dog and his boy. They spread their blankets on the cottonwood leaves that were probably at least 1 foot deep. Palmer told Andres, "Damn, boy, it's damn near like sleeping in a bed."

Before bedding down, they rotated their horses and relieved their bladders. As they lay in their blankets, Palmer and Andres looked up at the stars and Palmer asked Andres if he knew any of the stars. Andres told him that he could point out the moon when it was shining, but all he knew of the stars was that his mother was always telling him how pretty they were, to him they were just there. Palmer chuckled and agreed with him that they were just there and, as far as he could remember, they had always been there.

Palmer thought for a few moments about how he could relate to the young man about his own boyhood and growing up on the ocean front in Maine. He started by asking Andres if he knew what the ocean was. Andres replied that he had no idea. Palmer talked for some time about growing up in Maine and his brothers and him working on his father's small fishing boat. About how the ocean was saltwater and, how at night when you were out on the ocean, that sometimes the only way to find your way home was the stars. He explained how his father had been very adamant about his boys learning about the locations of certain stars. Andres was very skeptical about there being enough fish anywhere to fill a boat like Palmer was describing. Palmer laughed loudly and caused Chico to bark.

Palmer then told Andres about the little French trapper who was looking for passage back to France and how he had been skeptical about the stories the Frenchman had told everyone who would listen to him in the little Maine village. He told how he had left home against his father's wishes and had been amazed at the things he had seen in the first few years he had spent in the Minnesota wilderness. He also told him that he was still amazed almost every day by something that he saw or that happened to him.

Andres quietly asked Palmer, "Señor, what are we to do tomorrow."

Palmer sighed and replied, "We've got to be awful careful from here on and we got be ready for damn near anything. And listen, boy, you don't need to keep calling me, señor. How about Palmer?"

Andres said, "Por favor, señor, perhaps if you do not mind, I could call you Tio."

Palmer laughed and said, "Hell, boy, if that's what you want to call me, why it just suits the shit out of me." He put his hands behind his head. "Getting back to tomorrow, we have got to be getting close to Peña Blanca and according to what Mr. Peralta told us there are a hell of a lot of Benavides and Garcias. We both saw what they looked like that day and we can't afford to let them see us first. After what they did to Maria, boy, I got no problem shooting every one of the shiftless, no good bastards. Boy, I haven't ever had many folks treat me like family in a hell of a long time and I'm pretty goddamn particular about how they get treated and let me tell you that these sorry sons of bitches are going to pay for what they did."

After a moment of silence, Andres replied, "Si, señor, AH, I mean Tio."

Palmer told the boy, "Let's get some sleep and see what the morning brings."

Before daylight, Palmer was up and checked the livestock and relieved himself. He broke some twigs and added them to the coals from the night before and soon had a small blaze going. Going to the hole they had dug in the sand the previous night, he filled their kettle with water, satisfied his thirst, and then refilled the kettle. Returning to camp, he set the kettle in the fire and turned to the blankets where the boy and his dog lay watching Palmer move about. He picked up a stick and threw it at the two. The dog caught the stick while it was still in the air causing Palmer to laugh and say, "Come on, boy, you and Chico get up. We got some traveling to do and we've got to be careful about it."

After a breakfast of jerky and tea sweetened by a handful of sugar, they gathered their two saddle horses, put their saddles and gear on, and then packed the other one. Palmer let Andres pack their packhorse and, even though he had to tie up a hind leg, Palmer had to admit to himself that the young man was becoming quite proficient at quite a few things. Palmer said, "Damn, boy, you're making those critters do what you want."

Andres replied, "Gracias, Tio."

They mounted up and started down the river on a fairly good cart track. About midday, they came to a place where the track crossed the river and they could see an Indian pueblo across the river. The river was fairly high and appeared to be running pretty swift. Palmer asked Andres if he could swim but he wasn't even sure what Palmer was talking about. He had actually never been around enough water to have a reason to learn to swim.

Palmer dismounted and tied the packhorse's head to his horse's tail. He then told Andres to stay on his horse and to let him follow the other horses. He also told Andres not to panic if the horses started to swim, that his horse should follow him and the other horse. Palmer remounted and spurred his horse into the river.

Andres loudly said, "Tio, what about Chico?"

Palmer laughed and said, "Don't you worry about him, just take care of yourself." At about this time Palmer's horse stepped into the water and had to start swimming. Looking back, he said, "Come on, boy," and Andres rode into the river. The current carried them downstream about 100 yards below where the cart track came out of the river.

As Andres's horse lunged up the riverbank, the boy looked downstream and then over at Palmer with a panicked expression on his face. Palmer smiled and pointed downstream where a very wet dog was running towards them. Andres said, "Oh, thank you, Tio," and Palmer chuckled and said, "Hell, boy, that dog can take care of himself." He laughed out loud when Andres jumped off of his horse so that he could gather Chico in his arms.

Palmer dismounted and untied the packhorse from his saddle horse's tail. Andres and Palmer had held their firearms above the water, but Palmer told Andres that they should pull the balls from their firearms and recharge their powder charges just in case they had taken on some moisture. He said, "Damn, boy, it'd be a hell of a thing to run into those sorry bastards and have one of our guns misfire. Better to be safe." After recharging their weapons Palmer told Andres, "Boy, I want you to do what I tell you, I don't want you getting hurt. Pay attention to what I tell you and do what I tell you. I know that Maria Barcelo is not your mama, but she thinks that you are the closest thing to a son that she'll ever have and if something were to happen to you, you can bet that she'll skin my big ass for sure."

Andres looked at him with a rather bewildered look and said, "Que, why?"

Palmer shrugged and said, "She's a female, boy, a goddamn female."

They continued to the Indian pueblo where they encountered a priest. Andres was very nervous around the Indians even though the priest explained that they were in the Cochiti Pueblo and that the Indians were farmers and not violent at all. Palmer told the priest a little bit about what had happened to the young man many months prior and that he had good reason to be very cautious around Indians, Puebloans or otherwise.

Asking the priest about Peña Blanca, the priest told him that it was only about a 2 mile ride to the village. Palmer thought for a moment or two and then motioned for Andres to walk a short distance away from the priest.

He told Andres in a brusque manner that he wanted him to wait at the pueblo with the priest while he scouted out the village of Peña Blanca.

Andres said, "But Tio," but before he went any further Palmer said, "No, remember what we talked about, no arguing. I'll come back as soon as I find out anything." Returning to where the priest was standing, Palmer asked the priest if Andres could stay with him for a short time until he returned. The priest said the boy could stay with him.

Palmer then mounted and told Andres that he was going to leave the packhorse with him. He said, "Boy, I'll try to be back before dark. Take care of yourself."

"Tio, you must take care of yourself," Andres answered.

Palmer hadn't ridden more than a short time when he came into a clearing in which two men were starting to plow with a team of horses. Stopping to talk to them, he made small talk for a few minutes and then asked if they happened to know José Benavides. The two men suddenly quit talking. Palmer realized that he had probably screwed up. Raising his hand and saying thanks, he turned his horse down the trail towards the village of Peña Blanca.

Suddenly hearing a racket behind him, he stopped for a moment and one of the men who'd been plowing galloped by on one of the plow horses. Reining his horse to the side, Palmer let him go by. Sitting there on his horse, he was regretting mentioning José Benavides's name. He was thinking, *Goddammit, I bet those two are hooked up with Benavides or Garcia.*

His Harris rifle was on a leather thong hanging from his saddle horn and he reached down to gather it, when the other man came trotting down the cart track on the other horse. Palmer quickly checked to make sure that the percussion cap was still on the Harris's nipple.

Palmer Jackson: Yankee Mountain Man

As the other man trotted up on his horse, Palmer had his Harris cradled and his possibles bag with powder, shot, and percussion caps slung over his shoulder. When the man drew even with Palmer, he reined his horse up and smiled at Palmer. "Señor," he spoke, "you are causing trouble about Benavides. It is his brother who grew very excited when you asked, and I think that he is going to tell the village about you."

Palmer asked the man what he was doing as he was not in a hurry to get to the village. He replied that his name was Antonio Martinez and that he was not beholden to Benavides. He also stated that it was his opinion that Palmer should probably disappear as there would soon be several people coming to check on his whereabouts and they would not be too friendly, if things went true to form with the Benavides clan. Antonio Martinez then reined his horse back to the cart track and continued towards the village of Peña Blanca.

Palmer cursed loudly and rode back towards the Cochiti Pueblo. He had not ridden very far when his horse threw its head up and turned to look behind them. Palmer turned and could see several riders coming rapidly up the cart track. Palmer backed his horse off of the track and waited as the riders got closer, he recognized the man on the plow horse but didn't know the other two. He rode his horse into the cart track and had his rifle laying across his lap pointing in the direction of the approaching men. They got within talking distance and stopped.

One called out, asking, "You are the one called Palmer Jackson."

Palmer replied, "That's a true statement, mister."

The man replied, "You are the one who shot down my brother and my cousin and now you will pay."

Palmer asked, "Where is that coward, José Benavides—the one who kills women and children. What a sorry, son of a bitch coward he is."

The other replied, "Do not worry as he is on his way now and you will soon be screaming and begging for him to let you die."

Palmer thought, *What the hell? I'm in a bitch of a mess already, so I might as well start here.* He cocked the Harris rifle and pulled the trigger. The man in the middle that he had been talking to grabbed his right thigh and screamed. Palmer spurred his horse directly at them, pulling his pistol as he went. The man on the plow horse left in a run and the other man had a shotgun which discharged in the ground as his horse was plunging around in a circle. Palmer fired the pistol, striking him in the back. The man fell from his horse and lay still. Palmer was turning back towards the other man when he discharged his pistol, striking Palmer's horse. Palmer jumped from his horse as it was going down. When he hit the ground, he was running directly towards the man who had shot his horse. As he approached him, he punched up at him with his rifle barrel, striking him in the throat. He didn't want to use the rifle as a club because he couldn't afford to break it since he was very sure that he was going to need it again very shortly.

The man that he had punched in the throat fell off his mount and gagged and thrashed around on the ground. Palmer picked up a large rock and hit the man in the head as hard as he could. The man's mount was trying to shy away but Palmer caught him and tied him to a large willow. The next thing that he did was charge his Harris rifle and his pistol. He then retrieved the two dead men's firearms and reloaded them with powder and shot from their possibles bags. The shotgun and the pistol were flintlocks but still very usable. Sticking the pistol in his belt, Palmer then hung both rifles off of the second dead man's saddle and mounted his horse.

The horse danced around for an instant but as soon as he felt Palmer's spurs, he settled down and galloped up the cart track. A very short time later, Palmer could see a horse and a packhorse in a dead run towards him, with a brown and white dog following. Palmer pulled up and waited until the boy and the dog were there and then motioning them to follow, he rode off of the cart track and into a small incline with some trees. Reining up, he dismounted and told the boy to dismount also. They then tied their horses up and Palmer spoke quietly to Andres. "Boy, I thought that you were going to stay with the priest."

"Tio," Andres replied, "I heard gunshots and thought that perhaps you were in trouble so I came as fast as I could."

"That was not the agreement, but I'm glad that you came." Palmer related what had happened and told him that one had gotten away and probably warned Benavides about his presence.

Andres asked, "What can we do now, Tio."

Palmer told him, "We're going to sit right here and act like Indians and watch and see who goes by on that cart track."

The sun had moved about three quarters of the way across the sky when they heard horses coming. Motioning Andres to be quiet, they crawled out so that they could see the track. Soon five riders came into view, one of them was the man who got away on the plow horse. Palmer recognized another as the man who had shot at him in the cantina in Santa Fe. Anyone of the others could be a Benavides. Palmer and Andres remained quiet until the five men had passed out of sight. Palmer told Andres that the group would probably be back shortly. It wouldn't take long for them to realize that Palmer and Andres hadn't ridden through the Indian pueblo and left the area.

Palmer told Andres that it was very important that he not fire either of his firearms until he'd discharged all of his, including the dead men's shotgun and the flintlock pistol. He made sure that Andres checked his rifle and pistol, making sure that the percussion caps were on the nipples. Then, Palmer situated him in a hidden place behind a log with a direct line of sight to the cart track. He made sure that Andres's possibles bag with powder, shot, and caps was beside him. He then squeezed the young man's shoulder and left him behind the log. Palmer crossed the cart track and found himself a place where he could lay out his firearms and keep an eye on the trail. It was almost sundown when Palmer heard the horsemen coming back down the track.

Picking up the flintlock pistol and shotgun, he stuck the flintlock pistol in his belt with his pistol. He then carried his Harris rifle in his other hand. As the horsemen got closer, Palmer made sure that it was the same group. It was. And as they came abreast of him, he stepped out into the track, raised the shotgun one-handed, and shot Garcia, the man who'd shot at him in the cantina in Santa Fe. Garcia screamed and rolled off the back of his horse.

Then, Palmer raised the Harris rifle and fired at the closest one of the others. Knowing that he had hit him also, he dropped the shotgun and the Harris rifle and pulled both pistols from his belt. He cocked them and aimed them at the men on horseback. The flintlock misfired and when Palmer fired his own pistol at the man closest to him, the muzzle flash ignited the man's vest. Re-cocking the flintlock, he pulled the trigger again, but it misfired again and as he was trying to re-cock it the man on the plow horse ran directly over Palmer, knocking him to the ground.

At the same time, the remaining man jumped from his horse and straddled Palmer Jackson saying, "My name is José Benavides. I told you that you would pay for my brothers, and now you can die." He pulled a pistol from his belt. "Now you can die." At that instance, there was a gunshot, Benavides dropped his pistol, and he got a very funny look on his face. He slowly sat down by Palmer Jackson and the look on his face changed to frightened.

Palmer scrambled back onto his feet and he looked up at where Andres was. He waved for him to come down and then Palmer immediately gathered all of his firearms for recharging. When Andres got there, Palmer had him recharge his own firearms and his also. When Andres walked around the men, Benavides looked at him and then at Palmer and said, "A boy has done this to me, a boy."

Palmer looked at Benavides and said, "You're goddamn right a boy did that to you, a hell of a boy, and he is mine and the woman is ours, and you remember that as you lay there crying like a baby. Remember that nobody fucks with my family."

Benavides told Palmer, "You cannot leave me like this—I cannot move."

Palmer said, "You can kiss my ass, you sorry son of a bitching bastard. I hope you don't die for a week and scream your ass off the whole time. And remember to tell your people that if you fuck with Palmer Jackson's family—you can die."

Palmer and Andres each caught one of the dead men's horses. Palmer said, "Andres, we should probably get back to our horses and get the hell out of here before the other feller gathers another crowd of Garcias and Benavides." Then, he and the boy mounted their commandeered horses.

Riding up to where Andres's mount, packhorse, and dog were, Palmer and Andres dismounted. Palmer helped the young man gather his possibles bag and secure his belongings on the saddle. With his pistol in his belt, Andres mounted, reached down, and caught the pack horse's lead rope.

Palmer mounted, grabbed the reins of the spare horse, and led his group back up the cart track at a brisk trot. It was only a short time before the trio, Andres, Palmer, and Chico, arrived at the pueblo again. It was approaching nightfall, but they didn't stop. Palmer told the boy, "We'd better hit the river and put a few more tracks behind us." Andres only nodded and made his mount, which was pulling the packhorse, enter the water directly behind Palmer's horses.

The river floated them downstream again, approximately the same distance as it had that morning. Chico followed and was swept downstream and out of sight but, as the horses were clambering up the opposite riverbank, they heard the very wet and muddy dog bark before he burst out of the willows. Palmer chuckled at the dog, turned to Andres, and asked him if he was up to riding upriver. Andres answered, "Si, Tio, si."

Palmer turned his horse upriver, following the cart track and hit a brisk trot.

Quite a while later, he heard Chico bark. Palmer pulled his horse up and turned around. Andres's horse was riderless and the packhorse still followed. Palmer called sharply into the night, "Andres, where are you?"

Chico barked again from somewhere back down the track. Spurring his horse downriver, Palmer could just make out the white streaks on the dog.

CHAPTER FIFTEEN

Dismounting, he walked over to find the dog lying beside the boy. Squatting down by the boy, he asked, "Andres, what happened, what's going on?" The boy only groaned. Palmer reached down, got a hold of the boy, and realized that the young man was very wet and shaking uncontrollably. Palmer thought, *Goddammit, what the hell have I done to this boy?*

He walked to their packhorse, retrieved their blankets, and then covered the boy where he lay. Next, he tied all of the horses up. Then, he gathered twigs and dry grass and, after several failed attempts with his flint and steel, he added a small amount of powder from his powder flask and ignited them with a whoosh. Feeding more twigs and finally larger branches, he soon had a rather large fire crackling right in the middle of the cart track. Gathering rocks, he made a circle around the fire.

The river was only a short distance away, and he found a bare spot on the bank and dug a hole in the wet sand. While the hole was filling with water, he went to their packhorse and removed the pack. From in the pack, he removed a small kettle. He returned to the small hole that he had dug in the sand and filled the kettle about half full. He then returned to the fire and placed the kettle directly in the fire. He gathered more sticks and built the fire even higher. Palmer rummaged around in their pack until he located their tea and sugar. He dropped a very large pinch of tea into the kettle and then stirred in a handful of sugar with his knife.

While the tea was heating, he took a stick and rolled several of the stones away from the fire. After a few moments he could pick them up. He lifted the boy's blanket, laid the stones right next to Andres's body, and covered him back up. The boy was still unresponsive and shaking badly.

Palmer was thinking of things that he could have done differently and realized that he should have checked the young man after they crossed the river as it was snow melt and the night temperature was very likely freezing or lower than that.

As soon as the tea water started to steam a little, Palmer got a tin cup from the pack and filled it with the warm tea water. Sitting down by Andres, Palmer lifted him into a sitting position and attempted to pour some of the warm tea down his throat. Andres swallowed some and his eyes popped open. He told Palmer, "I am very sorry, Tio."

Palmer squeezed the boy tightly and said, "Boy, what the hell are you talking about? I'm the one that's sorry. I'm an old fart who has a lot to learn about boys and growing up."

He lifted the cup back to the boy's mouth. "Now, let's get some more tea in you and I have a few of Viola Silvas's tortillas left and some jerky. It's not much but we need to get some of it down you." While Andres was eating a tortilla and chewing some jerky, Palmer hauled some more warm rocks and noticed that Chico was under the blankets with the boy and that they both seemed quite comfortable.

Andres told Palmer that the warm rocks and the warm sweet tea seemed like the best thing that had ever happened to him. Palmer snorted and said, "Hell, boy, none of this would have happened if I'd not had my head up my ass."

Palmer Jackson: Yankee Mountain Man

The young man said, "But Tio, I need to stay with you, and I am very sorry that I caused this problem."

Palmer responded loudly and immediately, "Boy, what the hell did I tell you? I'm the one who's responsible for this problem and I apologize again for being an old fart who has forgot all about being a young man, and I would appreciate it if you could help me to remember."

Andres replied, "Si, Tio, and I want to go with you and to learn from you some of the things your father taught you and your brothers when you were young like me, things like using the stars to guide you on the ocean."

Palmer was silent for a time and then said, "Boy, I don't know a hell of a lot about anything, but how to get by, but you're sure welcome to anything that I know. Now, boy, I'm going to cut some willow twigs and, as you sip your sweet tea, I want you to chew two or three plum to pieces. They're going to taste kind of bitter, but it's going to make you feel better and take away some of your aches and pains."

After another cup of tea and chewing some willow twigs, Andres was able to get up and walk to the bushes and relieve himself. Palmer had him lay back down and surrounded him again with warm rocks and made sure that Andres and Chico both had another piece of jerky. It was not long before the boy's eyes closed and he was asleep.

After the boy fell asleep, Palmer got up and unsaddled all the horses and hobbled two of them, allowing them to graze. He would rotate them when he woke up in the night, allowing the other two time for grazing.

The sun was starting to come up when Palmer woke to find Andres and Chico already sitting up and watching him. Voicing a good morning, Palmer sat up and realized that he had an ache or two in his own body. He attributed these to being run over by the horse the day before. He asked Andres how he felt and was rewarded with a smile and two words, "Bueno, Tio."

Palmer told him that if he felt that good, he should rustle some twigs and grass and get a fire going for some tea. The boy gave another "Bueno, Tio" and sprang up, followed by Chico. In a few moments, Palmer was up and Andres had a fire going with a kettle of water heating. Palmer checked the horses and rotated them again. He relieved his bladder and then went down to the river and washed his hands and face.

He went back to the fire and dug in the pack and found the last of the tortillas and jerky. He asked Andres if he had washed his hands and received a shake of the head. He told Andres, "Boy, get down to the river and wash up. One thing I do remember is what a young man does with his hands as he's laying under his blankets. I'll fix us some tea and we'll eat the last of the tortillas that Mrs. Silva sent with us and chew some jerky also, if you're a mind to." They spent a short time eating and drinking tea, and then they gathered up the kettle and washed the sweet tea out.

Palmer rolled everything up in a small piece of canvas, and then Andres and he started saddling their riding stock. When they were through saddling their mounts, Palmer led the packhorse up and Andres quickly tied his left hind leg up and then put their sawbuck packsaddle on the horse and cinched it up. He then lashed their belongings down to the packsaddle. When he released the pack animal's hind leg, he didn't even buck.

Palmer looked at Andres and said, "Damned, if I don't think that you're getting that hardheaded bastard broke to pack." Andres smiled at him and bobbed his head in the affirmative.

Palmer said, "Boy, let's mount up and go to Santa Fe."

Andres grinned at him and said, "Muy bueno, Tio, muy bueno."

After mounting their horses and traveling for a short time, Palmer asked Andres how he was feeling, and the lad replied as long as they didn't have to swim the river that he was just fine. He asked, "Tio, do you think that we can travel all the way to Santa Fe today."

Palmer pulled his beard, looked at the boy, and grinned. "We'll have to ride like hell to make it today, boy. Do you think that you can handle it?" The young man grinned at Palmer and replied that he would like to eat supper with Mrs. Silva in her café.

Palmer told him to get his horse and packhorse up in front and hit a steady jog-trot. The boy kicked his horse into a brisk trot. The packhorse, Palmer on his mount, and the extra saddle horse followed. Chico ranged all around them on the cart track.

About midday, Palmer hollered at Andres to pull up for a short rest for the horses and them also. They dismounted and let the horses drink from the river. Andres tied up his saddle horse and the packhorse. He then found a sandy spot along the riverbank and dug a hole with a stick that began filling as soon as he quit digging. In just a short time it was almost full of clear water. Getting his tin cup from his saddle strings, he filled it with water and then offered it to Palmer who accepted it and drank with gusto. When Palmer lowered the empty cup, he then threw back his head and hollered, "Waugh! Goddamn, it's good to be alive, boy." Chico barked two or three times at him, and Andres laughed loudly. He filled the cup again and drank it down and then tried to imitate Palmer's holler, but it came out kind of squeaky and Chico barked at him and Palmer laughed loudly.

Palmer asked Andres how he was feeling as he himself could feel some aches and pains. Andres told Palmer that he was feeling fairly good considering what had happened the night before. The boy asked Palmer if he thought that they would make Santa Fe before nightfall. Palmer replied that they needed to get going again as he thought they still had a considerable distance to travel.

Palmer didn't want the boy to push himself too far as he thought that the young man was probably weak still from his ordeal of the night before. He'd decided that if he had the boy in front of him that perhaps he could tell if he began to waver and then he could call a halt.

For the two days Palmer and Andres traveled after the fight with the Garcias and Benavides, they didn't meet any travelers. Palmer and Andres drank as much water as they could hold, then they let their horses drink one more time. They started up the cart track once more with the boy in the lead. During the brief rest stop, both Andres and Palmer checked their firearms, making sure that the caps were on the nipples

Just about full dark of the second day, they stopped to water the horses and themselves and as they were standing there waiting for their water hole to fill, they heard a dog barking and—it wasn't Chico, as he was with them. Palmer told Andres, "Boy, that sounds like we're close to people. Do you want to go on or do we want to spend the night here?"

The boy replied at once, "Tio, if you would not mind, we could go on and see what is ahead of us."

Palmer said, "Hell, boy, let's get a good drink, take a leak, and see what's up ahead."

Andres grinned and said enthusiastically, "Bueno, Tio, bueno."

After getting a drink of water and emptying their bladders, with the boy in the lead again, they rode north on the cart track and suddenly they were coming up amongst buildings and lights. They reined over to allow a man driving six oxen hooked to a large cart to pass. Palmer asked the man where they were, but he couldn't understand him, so Andres asked the man where they were and he replied in Spanish, "Santa Fe." Even Palmer understood that, and he told Andres that they needed to find the livery stable where they'd spent the other night.

After a little searching they located the livery stable, but no one was around so Palmer and Andres went ahead and unsaddled and unpacked their livestock. Palmer then found a clean stall for their blankets. They washed in the large stock tank and then pumped fresh water over each other to rinse. Palmer told Andres that he thought perhaps Viola Silva wasn't ready for business as late as it was so they would try and find the cantina where he had eaten before.

With their pistols in their belts and their Harris rifles cradled in their arms, they started down the street in search of the cantina where they had eaten before. They turned into one and Andres said that he thought that it was the one. When they entered the conversation stopped, but suddenly someone shouted, "Señor Jackson and Andres. *Hola!* Hola!" and Joquine Peralta was there gripping both of their arms and pulling them towards a table. Telling them to sit, he went to the bar and told the bartender that they needed a cup of hot tea, one beer, and one glass of mescal. Returning to the table, he told both that they should relate their latest tales of their travels.

Palmer said, "Mr. Peralta we *will* be glad to tell you of our travels, but it's been sometime since we've eaten very much and we'd very much appreciate being allowed to eat first."

"Pardon, señor," Joquine stated, "I had no idea and please allow me to order you some food from the kitchen." Their drinks arrived and Mr. Peralta relayed to the bartender what their predicament was and that was soon solved with two large bowls of chili and a plate of tortillas.

Mr. Peralta pointed to the dog and he nodded yes, and the whole cantina laughed uproariously. Shortly after they started eating, the cook brought a pan of scraps out of the kitchen and sat them down by Chico who made them disappear.

Palmer again thought that the bowl of chili was actually a bowl of liquid fire. Andres appeared completely unconcerned about how hot the chili was and he actually asked for another bowlful—much to Palmer's amazement.

After they had finished eating, Joaquin Peralta asked Palmer if they had found Garcia or Benavides. Palmer told him that yes, they had found both Garcia and Benavides plus some of their friends. The barroom grew quiet and some of the men started to gather close to their table—even the bartender came from around the bar to hear the tale. Mr. Peralta told them to stand back and give them a little room. "Please, Señor Jackson, may we hear the story?"

Palmer said, "There's not a lot to hear, Mr. Peralta. We were on the way to Peña Blanca when we saw two men plowing in a clearing along the river. We then rode over, talked to them, asked about Garcia and José Benavides, and they said for us to go into the village. Then, we rode on and suddenly one of them burst by on a horse headed towards the village. The other man came riding by and told me that the other man was a Benavides and that there would probably be quite a few people coming to check us out." He then talked about both encounters as if Andres had been with him in both escapades.

When he was through, the bartender poured mescal for everyone, including Andres, and when everyone was ready Joquine Peralta shouted, "Salud, Señors Palmer and Andres Jackson." The rest of the barroom roared, "Salud, señors, salud!"

Chico was barking and men were walking by shaking Andres's and Palmer's hands. When things quieted down, Palmer went to the bar with the bartender and asked him how much he owed him. The bartender looked at him, smiled, and said, "Señor Jackson, the first time you came a man shot at you, and still you tried to pay me. The second time, I hear you and your son have made a bad man pay for his sins, and now you want to pay again. No, señor, not on this night."

Palmer thanked the man for allowing Andres and his dog Chico into the room to eat with him. "Never worry, señor," the bartender said, "they will be talked about for some time to come. And, please, señor, do come back when you come again to Santa Fe."

Palmer said, "You can count on it, my friend. The boy and I must leave, and I wish a good night to you, sir."

The bartender replied, "And to you and the boy also."

Going back to the table, Palmer told Andres to get his rifle and to call his dog because they needed to get some sleep as it had been a full and eventful day. As they stood to go, there were shouts for them to stay but Palmer told them that they must leave early the next day for Taos.

Going out into the night, Palmer and the boy turned towards the livery stable and some sleep. Palmer found a lantern and, after several tries, got some grass to burn and finally got the lantern lit. Making sure that the grass was extinguished, they entered the barn and found their clean stall. They took their boots off and lay down in the hay, then pulled their blankets over themselves, and turned the lantern off.

As they settled down, Palmer felt the dog slide between them. They lay there for a few minutes and then Andres spoke quietly, "Did you know that everyone thinks that I am your son?"

Palmer lay there for a moment before he answered. He said, "We have to do something about that, but I want you to know that I don't know a goddamn thing about kids, women, or families. I keep making mistakes and I'm afraid that I'll hurt you in some damn way that I couldn't live with."

"Tio, you and Maria Barcelo are my family and I do not want to be—how do you say?—without you."

Palmer reached over and got the boy's arm and told him that he didn't want to be without him either. "When we get back to Taos we'll sit down and talk about this with Maria."

The boy said quietly, "Gracias, Tio, gracias."

As Palmer lay there, he realized that he had some tears coursing down his face. *Holy shit*, he thought, *it's been about 40 goddamn years since any tears ran down my face. Thinking about the boy has damn sure changed the way I look at and do things.*

CHAPTER SIXTEEN

Daylight brought some activity to the barn with the owner feeding the stock and his children gathering eggs and playing. Palmer spoke to the man, explaining that it had been late when Andres and he had got there and that they had turned their stock loose in his large corral.

The owner walked over to the stall and looked down at Andres and told him that he should be up already because his dog had been up for some time helping his children gather eggs. Andres rose up on his elbow and called Chico. The dog barked and came running into the stall, jumping on top of Andres, licking and barking as though telling him that it was time to get up. Palmer looked at the owner and he was looking at Palmer and both of them laughed loudly.

Palmer told Andres to get up and that they'd try to rustle up something to eat. While Andres was pulling his boots on and rolling up their blankets, Palmer asked the livery man if he would be interested in buying one of their extra horses. The owner told him that horses were his business. They walked out into the big corral and Palmer pointed out the horse that he wanted to sell. The livery owner caught the horse and proceeded to look at his teeth, pick his feet up, and walk all around him. He then asked Palmer how many pesos he wanted for the horse.

Palmer replied that he would just as soon have American dollars or gold and that he thought that the horse should be worth a $20 gold piece. The livery owner turned to Palmer and said, "Señor, my name is Fidel Ortiz and I would like to know the name of the man who is attempting to rob me."

Palmer grinned and stuck his hand out and said as they shook hands, "Mr. Ortiz, my name is Palmer Jackson and the boy's name is Andres. We're going back to Taos and we need a little money to pay our way. If we could make a deal with you, I'd appreciate it very much."

The stable man kicked at some horse turds, scattering them around, and then said, "Señor Jackson, I can let you have seven dollars American or 11 pesos."

It was Palmer's turn to kick the horse turds and accuse Señor Ortiz of being a crook. He told him that Andres and he could live with $10 American or 15 pesos. Fidel Ortiz stuck his hand out and told Palmer that he could probably survive with this, but he would always remember him as a horse trader. Palmer grinned as they shook hands and replied, "I reckon that I feel the same way about you, señor."

After they gathered their remaining horses, saddled their riding horses and packed the packhorse, Palmer asked Andres if he thought that they should find Viola Silva's café and get themselves something to eat. At the mention of food, Andres quite agreed that they should find Señora Silva's café.

They left their horses tied up in Señor Ortiz's corral and went in search of the café. It was about three streets over, but they could have been blindfolded and located the café by the smells that were drifting in the wind. When they got to the café and entered, they were greeted by a young woman who was not Señora Silva. She told them to be seated and asked if they would like some hot tea. Andres and Palmer both responded that they would like some hot tea. The young lady brought two steaming cups of tea and told them that she had some chili with eggs over the top. Palmer told her that was fine with him and Andres nodded his okay also.

Before she could leave their table, Palmer asked about Señora Silva's whereabouts. The young lady smiled and informed them that Señora Silva was her mother and that her mother had been informed that her sister, who lived in Taos, had been attacked and injured. Her mother and father had left for Taos in their wagon to see if they could help her aunt.

Palmer and Andres looked at each other and about that time Chico barked at the door. The young lady went to the door to check and there was a brown and white dog sitting down, looking at her with his tongue hanging out. She gave a delighted laugh and said, "My mother told me of you three. You are Señor Jackson, his son Andres, and Chico."

Palmer looked at Andres and grinned and then said, "Yes, you're right."

She told Andres, "Please, invite your friend Chico to come in as he might be hungry also."

Andres smiled and motioned at Chico, and in he came and lay down between the two.

Palmer asked, "Miss, how is your mother's sister doing?" She told them the only news she knew, her aunt was injured—and Palmer and Andres had brought that information themselves four days prior.

Palmer asked, "You haven't heard anything else since then."

"No, señor," she replied, "but let me now get you something to eat." She returned in a few moments with a large platter full of tortillas with a bowl of honey and a large spoon. "Perhaps you can eat some tortillas and honey while I fix your eggs and chili?"

Palmer and Andres thanked her. Palmer with a thank you, and Andres with a "Muchas gracias, *señorita*." In a few more minutes, she came back with two large bowls of chili, one with two fried eggs on top, the other with three. She sat the one with two eggs in front of Palmer and put the three egg in front of Andres. She lay spoons down and told them to enjoy their meal. The young lady also told Palmer and Andres that her name was Maria and that she had been named after her aunt Maria in Taos.

As she was serving them, two men came in and sat down at another table. Seeing Chico laying there, they both laughed and told Palmer and Andres that they had been in the cantina last night and had enjoyed the telling of their travels.

When they were through eating, Palmer asked her how much they owed her and was rewarded with a loud "*Nada*, señor. My mother would be very upset if I collected money for your food after everything that you and your son have done for my aunt." Palmer thanked her and asked if perhaps they could get a few of the tortillas to last them through the day. And, of course, Maria said, "In a few moments." She came back with a paper wrapped parcel tied with some string.

Thanking her again, they prepared to leave, but she had to hug both of them before they could leave. When they arrived back at the livery stable, they put the tortillas in their pack on the packhorse. As they mounted up and rode out onto the street, Fidel Ortiz hollered at them to come back and see him again sometime. They both waved at the man and then spurred their horses into a brisk, ground-covering trot.

They only stopped twice all day and that was to relieve themselves and to water the horses. By nightfall, Palmer figured that they had probably covered at least half of the distance to Taos. They found a small stream that was running into the Rio Grande that was clear water and Palmer told Andres that they probably should stop for the night. Andres agreed and they unsaddled their horses and removed the pack from the packhorse. They then hobbled all three horses so that they could graze. Palmer told Andres that he thought that if the horses were as tired as he was that they weren't going anyplace because all they wanted was to graze on the grass.

The boy gathered several handfuls of dry grass and twigs. He then took Palmer's flint and steel and soon had a small blaze going that he fed larger sticks into to get a nice cheery blaze going. When it had burned down a little, he brought a kettle of water and set it in the fire. Then, he went to their pack and retrieved the package that Maria Silva had sent with them. Carefully unwrapping it, he sat up, and said, "*Meda*, Tio, meda." Palmer walked over and squatted down next to him and Andres showed him that the package not only contained some tortillas but a fairly large piece of cooked meat and four pieces of hard stick candy.

Palmer looked at Andres and said, "Damn, boy, there're some pretty good people around." Then taking his knife out, he gave it to the boy with instructions to cut them some slices of meat and that he'd make the tea. As they were eating their meat and tortillas, he asked Andres if this tasted any better than their jerky. Andres said that Maria's meat and tortillas was much better than the jerky. "But Tio, we must remember that the jerky made many meals for us."

"That's right," Palmer said, "but that doesn't make this meat and tortillas taste any less good."

Palmer told Andres that he thought that they had covered a good half of the distance and that if they got a good start in the morning they should reach Taos by nightfall. Andres replied sleepily, that it was "Muy bueno,

Tio, muy bueno." They lay down next to the fire and as soon as they pulled their blankets over them, Palmer felt Chico wiggle in between the boy and him.

It was an uneventful night and Palmer was up at daylight, more to relieve his bladder and bowels than being ready to go. He hadn't slept well since he'd worried about what was going to take place when they reunited with Maria Barcelo. What if she heard of everything that he had done and also exposed Andres to? He had to admit that the young man could have been hurt badly, maybe even killed.

Andres and Chico got up and walked into the trees and bushes and relieved themselves. Andres hollered across the clearing, "Buenos *dias*, Tio."

Palmer replied, "Pretty good, boy, pretty good." They got a fire going and heated the tea, had some more of Maria's tortillas and meat, then started packing up. The horses had done exactly what Palmer had said they would, which was spend the entire night filling up on grass.

Andres asked Palmer, "Taos today, Tio?" Palmer told him that if they made it to Taos, they were going to have to get hooked up and travel.

At midday, they stopped only long enough to water their horses and relieve their bladders. About an hour before nightfall, they topped a low hill and there was Taos, only a short ride down the mountain.

Andres was so excited that his horse even started prancing around and Chico started barking. Palmer told him to settle down and they'd get there in a short time. When they entered Taos and got to Maria Barcelo's cantina, they rode around to the back where her barn and corrals were. Octavio's children came running up and started talking and laughing with Andres. When they got to the barn and dismounted Palmer told Andres to go on and that he would take care of the livestock. He was almost through when he heard footsteps and turned around and there was Maria Barcelo with tears running down her face.

She approached him and, with her good arm, she encircled his body and squeezed him. She said as well as she could while sobbing, "You have come back to me. And young Andres also."

Palmer gently pushed her back from him so that he could look at her face and quietly said, "Maria, you might not want me back after you hear what I've done and let Andres do also."

She said, "Oh, Señor Jackson, you don't know how I have missed you and the boy. I do not care what you have done as you have done it for me." She wiped at her wet face. "Andres worried me greatly when he left but I knew that if and when he found you that you would take care of him. So, please, say nothing else about me not wanting you. I think that we can become a family."

"Maria, I want to talk to you about family," Palmer said. "Please, understand that I don't know anything about raising a boy and it's been so long since I've had a family or a home that I can hardly remember them."

Maria replied, "I have had no husband for almost 10 years, and I have no experience raising a child, so perhaps we could learn together, if you wish it to be so."

Palmer looked into her eyes and said, "I really do wish it to be so."

They heard some noise and turned. Viola Silva and Andres were standing there, and she said, "Men are such pendejos, a woman must take them by the hand and lead them. Without us they would wander by themselves forever. Andres, go to your *madre* and your papa." She then turned around and left the barn, shaking her head and muttering about how stupid men were.

ABOUT THE AUTHOR

John Snider grew up on a farm in the shadow of the Manzano Mountains of New Mexico. As a barefoot, *flaco* boy, he learned Spanish to communicate with his friends and keep up in school. So far in his life, he's trapped and hunted critters, worked as a mechanic, owned and worked a ranch, been a construction worker, served during the Vietnam War, and married a beautiful woman he proudly calls his wife. He's a proud papa and grandpa, too. *Palmer Jackson: Yankee Mountain Man* is his first published story.

Made in the USA
Middletown, DE
29 November 2024

65627875R00091